DEEP DUPLICITY

DEEP DUPLICITY

An Inspector Willis murder mystery by

Ray Klausen

AMARNA
BOOKS & MEDIA
www.amarnabooksandmedia.com

ISBN: 978-1-961869-11-0

Cover design by C. David Pina

Interior design: Thomas Edward West of Amarna Books & Media.

First print edition 2024

Amarna Books & Media
Philadelphia, PA
www.amarnabooksandmedia.com

Dedication

To John Harrington
A special and loving friend.
You are missed.

Acknowledgements

I wish to acknowledge the following people for their help and support in making this book a reality:

David Auerback
Naomi Gerbarg
Sean Grady, MD
Joann Grayson
Bree Halili
Philip MacKethan
Rich Miranda
H.R. Nicholson
Antoinette Peloso
Rebecca Sawyer Fay
Jacqueline Seyrat
Thomas Edward West

Table of Contents

Duplicity:

Deceitfulness or double-meaning

Chapter One
An Invitation Extraordinaire

Kimber Lepelletier could easily be labeled a "world traveler," as she had covered the globe as a writer and a woman who had an unending sense of curiosity and a taste for new adventures. Curiously enough, she was unfamiliar with the Cote D'Azur Airport in Nice, even though it served as the major link to Monte Carlo. In the past, she had visited Monte Carlo by train or car numerous times, but this was, in a way, a new experience for her.

In the past 21 years, she had lived in Paris in an exclusive apartment on Rue Logelbach, a highly desirable part of town.

To date, a continuous series of experiences created the outstanding woman who now walked off the plane and into the terminal.

Besides being remarkably attractive with just a hint of red in her luxurious long dark brown hair and her figure which was slim enough to make whatever she put on look remarkably special, she had an innate ability to exude a sexuality that gained the attention of most men and a sense of guarded awareness from most women.

She had been aware of this quality that was somehow built within her ever since she was 14 years old and discovered that the male sex found her irresistible and highly desirable. She never took this quality for granted, but used it subtly to get her way although it often had its price. She was aware that unless she was careful and guarded, it could get her into trouble.

Kimber was always alert and her antennae had been in overdrive from her first waking moment this morning.

She fingered the gilt-edged invitation that had arrived by special messenger to her home several weeks ago, and once again reread the card with a mixture of curiosity, amusement, and caution. It said:

Harding West requests your presence on his yacht
"Deeper and Deeper" for a ten-day cruise on the Mediterranean.
The cruise will start at The Yacht Club de Monaco in
Monte Carlo On July 10th

Guests are requested to bring the following attire:
Gentlemen: Beachwear, casual clothes,
sports jackets, and formalwear

Women: Beachwear, dressy sportswear as well as
formalwear appropriate for visiting
the Casino de Monte Carlo.

Enclosed is a first-class, round-trip air ticket to the
Nice Cote d'Azur Airport where a car and driver
will meet you and deliver you to the yacht.

R∫VP to Harding West 1-646 373995.

Kimber had mulled over this rather extraordinary invitation for several days and vacillated between accepting the invitation or politely rejecting it and filing it in a nearby wastebasket. But curiosity won out and she had called the phone number provided and left word with the man's secretary that she would gladly accept.

She had met Harding West at a dinner party given by

Fleur, a longtime friend of hers. It had been a small, elegant soiree that consisted of eight guests plus Fleur and her current companion, a handsome older gentleman named Maurice Calle, who was sophistication personified. While the other guests were interesting and full of delightful conversation, Kimber found herself drawn to an American named Harding West.

His rather remarkable good looks made him stand out in this small crowd. He was tall, maybe 6 feet 2 or 3 inches, which was a plus for her as she stood an elegant 5 feet 11 inches in heels, which often put her out of the running with many men she came across. His deep tan and pitch-black hair gave him sort of a leading man quality, but his manners and mode of behavior made it clear that he was different from the rest of the people at the party, and that fascinated Kimber. While Fleur had many intellectual and accomplished friends, this man was different. There was a strange mystery about him that was hard to define. *Fascinating*, she thought.

Fleur had everything set to perfection, from soft piano music in the background to delicious canapes that were passed around by her butler Claude as people talked in the salon. At 8:00 sharp, the two handsome paneled doors leading into the dining room opened and everyone was ushered into the elegant dining room, which consisted of an antique dining table with chairs covered in a French brocade surrounded by walls of carved wood panels from the 18th century. All this was illuminated by candlelight from a gilded, crystal chandelier and four matching wall sconces. There wasn't a sign of electrical illumination in sight. The table was laid with an antique lace tablecloth with a setting of Limoges china, Waterford crystal, pale lavender serviettes, and a unique flower arrangement of iris and violets that, while elegant, was low enough in height to not get in the way of conversations across the table. Fleur, as usual, had place cards so the guests were arranged to her liking, as she was brilliant at mixing her guests.

To Kimber's delight, she found herself sitting next to Harding and was amused to see him emulate the other gentlemen as they pulled out the chairs for the various female guests before sitting down themselves. While he might not be as sophisticated as the others at the table, he clearly was smart, aware, and a quick study… *very interesting.*

Included in the guests were Monsieur and Madame Prule, who were soon in a deep conversation with Maurice over the state of the current political scene in France and its standing with the world in general. It was a heated and contentious debate, with Madame Prule being particularly aggressive, which seemed to annoy her husband, as he was having a problem getting his thoughts included in the conversation.

That aside, dinner could not have been more enjoyable,

with a great deal of fascinating conversations, especially between Kimber and Harding, so much so that the evening flew by, and suddenly the party was winding down. To Kimber's delight and yes, to her surprise, he asked if he might call her, and she replied, "But of course," and proceeded to give him her number which he dutifully entered into his phone.

While Kimber was by nature usually guarded when it came to men making advances, she couldn't help but hope that this new acquaintance might move a bit forward, and she briefly fantasized as to if and how it might evolve.

The next day, Harding called at 10:00 AM and suggested that they meet for lunch. She reluctantly had to tell him that she was already booked, but perhaps they could meet for tea later that afternoon. He countered by suggesting tea at the Ritz where he was staying. *Well,* she thought, *clearly he's well off. I hope he's not one of those super nouveau-riche Americans who are full of themselves. But then he had been so very polite and more interested in me than in talking about himself last night. Time will tell.*

That afternoon, she arrived at the Ritz expecting to have to call up to his room to announce her arrival. There was no way she was going to go up to his room, but to her surprise and delight, he was standing outside the lobby. He obviously had been waiting for her and was filled with smiles. They shook hands, with him holding on just a bit longer than one normally would, which strangely didn't bother her at all. He had a medium-sized folded umbrella hooked over his arm. She gestured towards it and asked, "What's that for?" as there was not a sign that it would be raining in the near future.

He grinned and gestured down the street and said, "There was a poor man back there who was selling these umbrellas and I felt sorry for him."

Interesting, she thought. Looking it over she saw some printing on the fabric. "What does that printing say?" she asked.

To which he shrugged, "No idea," and with that he proceeded to open the umbrella to reveal the words in bold letters: "*MERDE, IL PLUIE.*"

Kimber grinned and said, "Do you know what that means?"

Harding shrugged, grinned and said, "Not a clue."

"Well, it's a bit vulgar but amusing… It says 'Shit, it rains!'" to which both laughed loudly, to the amusement of the people around them.

With that, Kimber said, "Shall we?" as she said motioned for them to go in for tea. He quickly folded the umbrella and offered her his arm. She later found out that it was a motion he had once seen in a movie, had been charmed by it and consequently emulated the gesture. As they walked into the Bar Vendôme with its red velvet banquettes and spotless white linen tablecloths, everything was impeccably correct. With its famous Belle Epoque glass roof, it embodied the elegance of the Ritz itself while soft music played in the background. The setting was perfect for *un rendezvous de deux personnes.*

While Kimber had been to the Ritz often, she sensed that this meeting somehow seemed to have a special air. Clearly, this was to be a unique experience for Harding, but instead of projecting a sense of nervousness or, worse yet, showing off, he was merely excited about meeting her and was thrilled with her and the place itself. He was charming and disarming.

"Have you been to this place before?" he asked as they were seated.

"Actually, quite a number of times. A good friend used to take me here often."

Harding seemed a bit disappointed by this bit of information, as clearly he wanted to impress her and to make this meeting special. Sensing this, Kimber said, "You have no idea how wonderful having tea here is for me as it brings back so many treasured memories and the wonderful times I spent here with René. I should explain: René was the love of my life. I met him—what…"

She paused and mulled it over. "It must have been 18 years ago. We were inseparable. He was married but had been separated from his wife for a number of years. She was a devout catholic and refused to give him a divorce, so eventually we came to an agreement where we lived together as man and wife but without the papers to make it legal. I was fully accepted by his father, and the three of us used to go to Monte Carlo often at the height of the season. In those days one always dressed when going out and especially to the Casino. His father used to tease Claude and say, 'You need to spoil Kimber a bit,' and I ended up receiving some rather impressive jewelry and a fabulous wardrobe, not to mention adventures as a result of his prodding."

"Mind you, I was my own person, having made excellent money on my own, but oh, how wonderful it was to be fussed over and deeply loved by someone truly special. Unfortunately, he died two years ago and…" She made a gesture of frustration and loss and left it at that.

Harding was mesmerized by this enchanting woman. Not only was she stunning-looking and clearly intelligent, she also projected a warmth and charm that made him want to spend as much time with her as he could.

"Enough about me," she said. "Tell me about you."

"Let's save that for another time," he said, hoping that the suggestion might result in more time together. "Tell me what you've been up to."

"Oh, I've been proofing a friend's novel, as she respects my ability in that area. Normally this is a risky thing to undertake as, what does one do when a book is truly *horrible*?

But in her case, she's a fine writer and it is a pleasure to help her out. And I must say, I've had a few suggestions to propose to her," she said with a grin. "I've also been working on recovering a chair in my salon. I enjoy working with fabrics and this project is particularly challenging... Perfect for me."

And so, the afternoon went on longer than either had intended, and it could not have gone better. He appeared to be genuinely interested in her and not at all full of himself. In fact, it was difficult for her to find out much about him. as he would repeatedly move the conversation back to her. Consequently, the talk was mostly about her. She found that unique and charming and, yes, she wanted to get to know more about him. At the end of their tea, he asked in the most disarming and unassuming way if he might see her again, and to her surprise, she suddenly suggested that maybe he might enjoy a simple French dinner at her place the next night.

At first, he started to say that he was tied up and expected back in Monte Carlo, but suddenly he changed his reply to "Hey, why not? I was expected at a business dinner then... but I'll just change it to the day after", followed by a charming grin. While she had given him her phone number the night before, she now gave him her card with her address and phone number, which he looked at with interest and took his time to put it safely away.

He explained that a while ago he had some business dealings with a few Japanese businessmen and had learned that to quickly shove a person's business card into one's pocket was deeply insulting, and so he had developed the habit of studying a business card carefully, and then at a quiet moment carefully slipping it into his pocket. After doing this, he gave her a kiss on both cheeks and said, "I've seen others do that here in your country. I hope it's ok with you."

To which she smiled and said, "It was *trés parfait*." And they each walked away in opposite directions. However, on impulse, Kimber looked back just as he turned around and gave her a little wave, which she returned. Despite her usual precautions, she was enchanted and disarmed.

The next evening, Kimber cooked a *poulet*, a simple French dish she had learned from her mother. Earlier she had gone a short way over to the local market to pick up a fresh chicken, and on the way home, on impulse, she bought a small bouquet of white peonies with peach centers to dress up the table. She also bought a *tarte* from her favorite patisserie.

Harding arrived at her apartment just off Parc Monceau in the chic 8th arrondissement, with its Egyptian pyramid, Corinthian pillars, a Venetian bridge and a Chinese pagoda—created in the 17th century by order of the Duke of Chartres—with its stately 200-year-old trees. This was so foreign to him and truly exciting. Harding rang the apartment bell outside the massive building door and soon was buzzed into a small courtyard where he found another set of doors, glass this time, which were impeccably clean.

He found and proceeded to buzz a new apartment, number 2 on the étage 4. This, he surmised, meant the 4th floor. This was quickly returned by a click indicating that the door had been unlocked. He went through the heavy glass doors and entered a very small elevator which took him noisily up to the 4th floor.

She stood waiting for him so she could guide him towards her apartment. As the elevator cage moved up to her floor level, she saw Harding appear with almost a silly boy's grin on his face... charming even though he was clearly in his 40's. The elevator gate opened with its usual rattle and creak of steel-to-steel movement and, to her amusement, he presented her with a beautiful bouquet of peonies. She looked at the floral paper around the flowers and quickly recognized that they came from the same flower shop just down the street where she had bought her bouquet.

As he entered the apartment and saw her flowers on the table, he muttered something about "great minds" and they both laughed. Even though he clearly came from a different world, they seemed in many ways to be on the same wavelength. It was fun to be with him and, yes, *trés unique.*

Harding looked around the living room which, he soon learned, she referred to as "the salon." It had a high ceiling with walls covered in a soft peach fabric and had paneled doors with exquisite, gilded hardware which led to other parts of the apartment. There were many unusual antiques throughout the apartment and the floors of the apartment were handsome polished parquets covered with rich oriental rugs. On one wall there were three tall windows which looked out on the apartment buildings across the way. Each window had a very small exterior balcony with a handsome wrought iron railing with a simple but elegant pattern. On each balcony were flowerpots filled with peach-colored geraniums.

Clearly, she was partial to this color. When Harding admired the room and especially the fabric covering the walls, Kimber grinned a bit and proudly explained that in France one could buy fabrics that were very wide and since she loved to sew and work with fabrics, she had applied a batting, a form of padding to the walls and then covered it with the peach fabric. The fabric was "railroaded" around the room without a seam in site. This astounded Harding as he couldn't quite imagine how this woman had managed that.

"Surely you had help," he said

To which she said simply with a shrug, "No, I did it all by myself. I'm a bit of an independent woman and I love challenges."

Harding was deeply impressed.

"I saw that you had a lot of framed photos in the entry

when I came in. Family?" he asked.

"Yes, While I have never been married, I have quite an extensive family thanks to my three brothers, but no children of my own. Also, a great many of the photos are of my friends who represent the real wealth in my life. Someday maybe you'll meet some of them." *Hmmm, that sort of slipped out,* she thought. *I hardly know this man and yet...*

She quickly set about putting his flowers into a handsome crystal vase which she put on the marble mantelpiece.

"There, don't they look *superbe*?" Harding had to agree.

She then offered him a drink which ended up being a Kir, technically a Kir Royale, which she made from champagne with some creme de cassis added to it, giving it a beautiful peach-like color. She offered it in an elegant champagne glass and then made one for herself. With that she said, "Of course if you don't like this, just let me know as I have most other drinks... scotch, bourbon, gin, just name it."

But Harding took one sip and nodding his approval said, "How did you say it... *superbe*?"

Kimber thought: *now wouldn't this be the ideal time to find out more about this charming man?* and so she said, "To date I've told you quite a bit about myself. Now how about letting me in on who you are?"

And so, he started to explain who he was, which was a bit of a challenge as he definitely did not want to come off as bragging or being full of himself. He slowly began.

"I was born in New York to a lower-middle-class family on the South Shore of Long Island. We had one of those uninspired ranch-type homes left over from the Post-World War II boom. Nothing special, but it was on a canal and so at an early age I was given a little boat, nothing to brag about."

"Over the years I worked delivering newspapers, was a busboy in Jones Beach, and so forth. Simple jobs to earn some money. It's what boys did under those conditions where there wasn't family money to go on vacations or to play the summers away at the beach. However, I had my boat which I used for clamming, which proved to be quite lucrative and kept me in shape." To which Kimber couldn't help but admire his strong shoulders.

"I had some wonderfully buddies. A guy named Dick Harper, who unfortunately died way too young, and an amazing guy named Harvey Willis, who we all called Willis. You'd love this guy… so smart. When he grew up, he became an inspector in the police force but is now retired and head of a private investigating company. You should hear some of his stories!"

"Anyway, over time, my love of boats grew, but my monetary resources somewhat limited me in terms of getting a decent-size boat. I was lucky in that I had very good test scores for getting into college and I ended up going to Harvard on a scholarship. However, despite the scholarship, I graduated with a considerable debt which I was determined to pay off as soon as I could. And I did. My background is in finance, and it turns out that I'm just a natural at it. I can smell when a stock has a special potential… is going to take off and I'm good at buying low and holding on as the stock grows and grows. I worked for a number of years at Morgan Stanley and was one of their top producers, but hated being part of a large organization, so I eventually left and went out on my own. Over the years I did quite well and built my own company and the company grew and grew."

"Over time I built a team and made a ridiculous amount of money on stocks that took off. Stocks such as Apple, Microsoft, Netflix, Amazon, Facebook, Google, Goldman Sachs, J.P. Morgan, and Monster Beverage. Of course, I bought some stocks that were duds, but not many. I used to tell my clients when they would panic if the market went down that the only people who get hurt on a roller coaster are the ones who get off when it's moving."

"Luckily, most of my clients listened to me and in the end, I did very well for my clients and also for myself," he said with kind of a boyish grin. "In all, we're talking about an obscene amount of money that I've made during these times. I hope this doesn't sound like bragging. It's just how things evolved for me."

Kimber smiled, as it was refreshing to be with a man who, while obviously very successful, had a sort of boyish, modest streak which she found quite irresistible.

"It was during these years that I met and married a fine woman named Phyllis. She was in her mid-20's and I was in my early 30's. Sad to say, the marriage didn't last, as she was jealous of my love—my company—and we just somehow couldn't make the marriage work. We tried to adjust and change so our lives would mesh better. We even went into counseling, but I don't know, maybe it just wasn't meant to be. I probably was just too ambitious, too focused on my work, and just not ready for a meaningful relationship. I think when she had the miscarriage, that certainly didn't help matters. I thought I was being supportive but clearly, I wasn't, and so we drifted apart."

"Phyllis tried to understand, but somehow the spark that we felt when we first met fizzled out. Sad, in that I still care for her, I just don't love her, and she clearly has moved on. It's kind of strange in a way, as I've seldom failed at anything. That marriage was, however, devastating for me and one that still hurts to this day. Anyway, in the end, we decided to end it amicably, if there is such a thing."

"We even used the same lawyer which, in retrospect, I'm not so sure was a great idea. In any case, since she was financially well off to begin with, Phyllis didn't take much of a bite out of our mutual finances. I think she was just so bummed out that she couldn't make me love her enough to stay in the relationship in a way that fit her needs and ideals. And so, she just wanted out."

"She was a smart, stunning woman and felt she wanted a better man in her life, one who would devote more time towards her and a marriage. As we all know, there tends to be a feeling on the part of many women that there's a clock ticking... There is the question of finding the right man while the woman is young and attractive so she can build a nest and start a family. At the time I didn't really understand this. I just thought... Well, how would I put it? Maybe I just didn't think of her side of things. I was just so focused on my company and making it big and strong. She has since met someone, got married and the last thing I heard was she was pregnant."

"Well, after the divorce, I totally submerged myself with my work, and ended up succeeding beyond my wildest dreams. Then one weekend, on a lark, I went to a boat show and seeing all those fantastic boats and all the smiling people who clearly were excited about their passion for boats made me think... There I was in my early 40's with my work being my only passion. There had to be more to life than work, I thought. There had been a group of men who wanted to buy my company, but I had sort of blown them off... but, of course, in a polite way. My uncle, whom I adore, had just suffered a heart attack and while he survived, it underlined the fact that we're all mortal. So, I put out some feelers out to see if there was still any interest for someone to buy my company, and my timing was perfect."

"There were actually two companies which wanted to buy me out and, well, there was sort of a bidding war, and I came out way better than I had expected. It was around this time that I read a New York Times article about several executives who had taken off several months each and found that in addition to relieving stress, the time away allowed them to ignite creativity, develop 'out of the box' thinking. This was a very exciting thought for me. Maybe I could sell my company and create an exciting new life for myself. And that's exactly what I did."

"Selling my company gave me a whole new way of looking at life. While I was now extremely comfortable, I had no focus in life. My work had become my whole core of existing and now, with the exception of the two years while I've stayed on with the company in a consulting position, I'm now starting to build a life that will hopefully keep me creative, and yes, content. That said, I'm finally taking the time to make friendships which I hope will last me the rest of my life. I also have a new toy, a boat named 'Deeper and Deeper', which I want to share with my friends. and I'm hoping you might come and see it one of these days... maybe share some time with me on it."

And so, he concluded the evening by saying, with a twinkle in his eye, "What a '*superbe*' evening it has been."

Two days later, he called her and asked if she had any

interest in antiques, to which she replied, "Well, wasn't that a bit obvious when you looked around my salon?"

"I understand that Paris had some outstanding flea markets. Do you know them and are they any good?"

"But of course. There's *Les Puces*. which is the largest of its kind in the world, and it simply overflows with vintage and antique treasures. It's located at Porte de Clignancourt and is officially called *Les Puces de Saint-Ouen*, but everyone knows it as *Puces* or "The Fleas". Why do you ask?"

"Well," Harding said as he scratched his chin, "If you saw my home in New York, you'd see that I'm also very into antiques. I love collecting them."

"In that case, you'd love *Les Puces,* as it covers seven hectares or a bit above 17 acres. It's open every Saturday to Monday year-round. Would you like me to show you around?"

"Are you kidding? I'd LOVE it!" he said with great enthusiasm.

"Excellent, Harding. If you're free, we could go early this coming weekend. I would recommend that we go on Saturday or Sunday as many dealers aren't open on Monday."

"Sure," Harding replied with a grin into the phone.

"Why don't you pick me up at say 7:00 AM this Saturday so we can have a leisurely café crème and watch the antique world set up? We could take the Metro, and head to Porte de Clignancourt on Line 4. I must warn you to make sure your wallet is secure and do NOT bring your passport.

While the area is basically safe, there are a number of pick-pockets who work the market."

And so, it was agreed that he would pick her up that Saturday morning. He suggested that they take his car as he had a driver at his disposal, but Kimber said, "No, *mon Cheri*, the Metro is quite easy and the parking in Porte de Clignancourt is *trés horrible*."

And so, the date was made.

That Saturday, he buzzed her apartment, and she was down and out the main door within moments. She was dressed very casually in tan slacks and a sweater with a light jacket in a soft green that picked up the green in her eyes.

The first thing Kimber said was, "Have you secured your wallet?"

"Yup, I heard your warning and I'm keeping it in the pocket in the front of my pants and will keep my hand in that pocket most of the time per your advice, Madame," as he gave her a mock salute.

She smiled and took his arm as they set out for the Metro. When they got to the station and went down the steps, she produced two Metro tickets, so Harding didn't have to go through the process of buying tickets for the two of them. He objected, saying, "I should take care of our tickets."

Kimber scoffed, "Don't be absurd, *mon cheri*, it's nothing and if it will make you feel more comfortable, you can treat me to the *café crème* when we get there."

The ride on the Metro was a pleasure, as the Paris trains turned out to be remarkably quiet because the trains travel on rubber tires compared to the noisy subways in New York which use steel wheels on steel rails. Harding used the New York subway from time to time when he was in a rush and needed to go a considerable distance, but this was unique to him and an unexpected pleasure.

Because they were deep in conversation, they almost didn't get off at their stop. When they did, Harding noticed that the neighborhood was considerably less affluent than where Kimber lived. Really no surprise there. He soon noted that the individual markets setting up tended to run into each other, and it was not obvious where some shops stopped and others began.

Kimber soon directed him to where they could get their *café*, which was served steaming hot along with two delicious straight croissants. When Harding remarked about how delicious the croissants were, Kimber said that the straight croissants legally must be made with butter, hence the delicious and consistently wonderful taste.

Soon Kimber reached into her shoulder bag and produced a map that contained an excellent directory of dealers and helpful information. After perusing the map a bit, with Kimber pointing out some potential points of interest, they started out along Rue des Rosiers.

There they saw several interesting shops selling Art Deco furniture, fireplaces, mirrors, and decorative furniture. Kimber said, "I've bought several mirrors and some furniture at the second dealer over there on the right. They have a great selection at very reasonable prices. Further down on the left, before Serpette, there's a shop that sells interesting decorative pieces, including paintings and garden pieces, and so forth."

A bit on, she pointed out Marche Vernaison, 99 Rue des Rosiers and the smaller Marche Antica. Vernaison was a wonderful, winding market which carried anything from furniture to beads, to textiles, paintings, antique toys, and more. The latter delighted Harding, as it turned out that he had a small collection of antique toys in his New York apartment.

He selected a windup toy of the Queen Mary and asked the price. When told, he took out his wallet from his front pocket and counted out the number of Euros the proprietor requested. Kimber smiled, as she was used to bargaining for such purchases. She was about to suggest that he try to get a better price but realized that to him it was a small amount, and it wasn't worth mentioning and possibly ruining the joy he just had with his purchase.

As they walked on, he said, "I love collecting antique toys. I've been looking for a period toy of the Queen Mary forever. Did you know that the Queen Mary was launched in 1934 and as part of the celebration, they made small metal models of that boat that same year. They are impossible to find but today, thanks to you, I was finally able to buy one. Just look at it!" he said as he held it up for her inspection. It was made of metal, maybe eight or so inches long, was red and black with a white deck, had portholes and three red smokestacks with a key sticking out of the center one so one could wind it up, set it in the water, and sail it.

"Amazing… The thing is I had one just like it as a small child. And I loved it! I was maybe seven or eight and I was at Jones Beach with my folks. As I tried to sail it, a big wave came up and took my boat away. I was distraught, but my mother, being the wise, sensitive woman she was, said, 'Don't cry, it's probably on its way back to Europe where it came from. Someday it will return to you.' And now I have it once again. It's back thanks to you!" They both smiled at the thought and the pleasure they just shared compliments of Kimber and her antique dealer.

Shortly after, as Harding looked at his new toy boat, he said, "I have a rather larger boat which I keep in a yacht club in Monte Carlo. Would you consider coming there as my guest along with some other friends of mine and spend some more time with me?"

Kimber tilted her head as if taking the offer in, and finally said, "We'll see."

Later, as they walked on, Kimber said, "You know, part

of the fun when shopping here is to try to get a lower price. For example: what we should have done is have me declare in a loud voice that the toy was '*Trés cher… too expensive.*' That way the dealer might think he'd lose the sale and might very well have offered the toy at a lower price. Nothing offered… nothing gained. That's the fun part. I love the game!"

Harding looked at her, first with surprise but then amusement, and at the next vendor, he asked the price of an antique pocket watch. When the dealer named a price, he looked at Kimber and said, "What do you think, Honey? Isn't it beautiful?"

To which Kimber said, without batting an eye, "I don't think so, darling. Besides, you have way too many watches already."

With that they kind of stared at each other and the proprietor said, "Please, Madame, it's such a beautiful piece and Monsieur certainly would enjoy having it in his collection. I think I could let it go for 20 Euros less."

To which Harding said, "Aw, please, Sweetheart, just this once?"

Kimber stared at the watch and finally sighed deeply and said, "OK, but just this once."

Then with the biggest grin Kimber had ever seen, she saw Harding take out his wallet and pay for the watch. As Harding held the watch in his hand, he said, "You have no idea how much I will treasure this, sweetheart," and he gave her a big kiss before taking her arm. Leading her away, both tried unsuccessfully to stifle their laughter.

Later, on the train ride back to her place, they saw two young thugs get in the way of an obvious tourist who was trying to get off the Metro. There was a tussle and Harding saw the man's passport fall to the floor of the train. The man had just had his wallet pickpocketed and, in the process, his passport had slipped out of his pocket. The man was oblivious to it and went out the train door. Harding quickly grabbed the passport and threw it to the man just before the Metro door closed. The two thugs quickly ran into the next car and got away. After discussing the incident, Kimber and Harding surmised that the tourist would hopefully realize that his wallet had been pickpocketed and would hopefully report his loss to the police and cancel his credit cards. Kimber had been right about urging Harding to keep his wallet safe in his front pocket.

Clearly, they were getting along better than either one had hoped, and so, the next day, it was agreed that she would seriously consider his offer of joining him on his yacht. We'll see, she thought. Little did she know what she was getting into.

Chapter Two
Monte Carlo

A fortnight later, she found herself on her way to Monte Carlo and deplaned in the Nice Cote d'Azur airport. She soon spotted a man in white livery holding a sign that said, "Mademoiselle Kimber Lepelletier." Kimber walked up to the man and said, "*Bonjour, Je suis Mademoiselle Lepelletier.*" To which the man saluted and said with a clipped British accent, "How was your flight, *Mademoiselle?*"

Kimber replied, "*Trés bon…* short and easy. Thank you for asking."

"Please," the chauffeur said as he gestured for Kimber to

follow him to the baggage claim area. She easily spotted her pieces of luggage, which were the first to arrive on the carousel. He quickly secured a luggage cart and led the way to an impeccably clean white Rolls Royce in the nearby parking lot.

The chauffeur held open the door to the back seat of the car and as Kimber got into the car, she said lightly, "Obviously, you know my name. May I ask what's yours?

The chauffeur replied with a little salute. "My name is Mac, *mademoiselle*. At your service." Kimber nodded politely and said, "*Merci* for meeting me." And off they went.

While Kimber normally traveled light, she was extra careful to pack enough of a wardrobe selection so that she would be prepared for any occasion. This included a number of casual clothes suitable for on deck and daytime wear for offshore excursions, 10 evening outfits ranging from elegant casual to very dressy with matching shoes and purses, as well as a selection of sweaters and jewelry.

From experience she knew to bring some fine accessories, necklaces, bracelets, etc., but nothing of great value. There was, however, one piece that was called a "travel necklace" that looked extraordinarily valuable but was, in fact, an exceptionally fine piece of costume jewelry. One would need a jeweler's loupe to tell its true value. All of this had been packed in the five pieces of cream-colored Bellagio V2.0 luggage, plus she had a small carry-on case which held her makeup, a small amount of medications, her pa-pers, and her jewelry. She was well equipped physically for the days to come, but emotionally it remained to be seen with what lay ahead.

The drive to the yacht was uneventful and enjoyable in that the weather was perfect, a welcome change from the last four rainy days in Paris. The chauffeur had obviously called ahead, as Harding was standing on the stern of the yacht and was smiling eagerly. He stepped off the deck as the chauffeur opened Kimber's door and quickly walked over and gave her once again a warm embrace and a kiss on each cheek. *Hmmm, very European,* she thought with amusement.

The yacht was 41 meters or approximately 134 feet long and was moored in the exclusive Monaco Yacht Club, a pri-vate club founded by the late Rainier III, Prince of Monaco, the husband of Grace Kelly.

"How was your flight?" he asked. "Smooth, I hope."

She replied, "Just so-so," with a shrug.

Ignoring her reply, he enthusiastically said, "I told you that there would be other guests coming on board but they're scheduled to arrive tomorrow, as I wanted more one-on-one time with you before the others arrived. Of course, if it's uncomfortable for you to be my sole guest tonight, I'll certainly put you up in a nearby hotel."

"Oh, that won't be *nécessaire*. I appreciate it but after

all, I've traveled the world all by myself and I can take care of myself."

"Come let me show you your new home away from home. As you know, the yacht is called the 'Deeper and Deeper,' and, believe me, it is making a nice dent into my retirement funds," he said laughingly. His excitement was contagious. Clearly, he was proud of his boat but not meaning to brag about his wealth. In a charming way he was almost like a kid with a new toy... *Some toy*, she thought...

The yacht was extraordinary. It was gleaming white with sleek lines and accents of pear wood flooring and paneling throughout. The decks were incredibly shiny and pristine. It looked as if no one had ever used it.

"Would you like a tour or perhaps you'd like to settle into your cabin first?" he asked. "It's up to you."

"You're the captain, Sir," she replied as she gave him a mock salute and they both laughed. His excitement over the boat was incredibly contagious. And so, after one of the stewards offered each of them a Kir Royale, Harding winked to her as they crossed over the rear deck and entered the rear salon. The salon was amazingly large with its handsome paneling that glistened in the light coming in from the many large side windows.

The furniture consisted of a number of modern white chairs and sofas upholstered in kid leather, with blue cushions that picked up the blues in the various modern paintings and prints that were mostly framed in the same wood as the paneled walls. At the end of the room was a u-shaped bar with a white marble top with crystal glasses and other bar type equipment on the shelves below. On top of the bar was a crystal ice bucket with an ice pick with a horn handle and ice at the ready.

A wide opening just next to the bar led through to a second salon, which featured a selection of furniture in white with accents of blue from several toss pillows. The color echoed the blue in the artwork and gave an undeniable richness to the surrounding walls.

Some of the pieces were modern art and some nautical in nature. Included in the furnishings was a large sofa, a gaming table with six chairs, and a collection of games neatly stored in a cabinet nearby. Across from the sofa and beyond that was a glass dining table with 12 chairs, again covered in the same blue fabric. There were arrangements of flowers here and there, mostly in white with an occasional accent of blue irises.

Beyond it was the kitchen, which Harding referred to as the "galley". It was pristine with its white granite counter tops, stainless steel six-burner stove, and two extremely large refrigerators, again in stainless steel. Everything was spotlessly clean and simply arranged. Beyond was a small area that had an additional small sink that appeared to be for preparing food and for handling the cleaning up of dishes, as there were two dishwashers on one wall.

Harding then led her through a doorway into what he called his office, which was in fact a rather large room with more paneled walls with bookcases and a desk, plus a sofa and two chairs which were covered in a light blue-grey. Kimber noted the low railings around the bookshelves which appeared to have the sole purpose of containing the contents on the shelf in case of high seas. The room was quite pristine, very comfortable and efficient, but lacked any personal touches such as photos or memorabilia of Harding's life.

Beyond it, and on a higher level, was the helm station or bridge which was where the captain and his assistant piloted the yacht. All the controls were chrome and gleaming, and the area was impressive in its array of controls for sailing the boat. Back towards the stern was an indoor/outdoor entertaining space with wood decking that looked like narrow strips of polished teakwood with a number of tables and chairs, some with high tops so one could more easily see out over the surrounding windows. This area could easily entertain two dozen guests.

The deck continued towards the stern or the back of the boat where there were numerous pieces of lounging furniture, again in blues and whites ending with a round Jacuzzi about eight feet in diameter and two jet skis which were covered in white canvas to protect them from the outdoor elements.

Harding then led her down a narrow, carpeted staircase with wood handrails on either side that led to the crew quarters. These were set up to handle six in crew in three separate cabins. Here and there one could see personal photos of what Kimber assumed were of the crew's family and friends. All was very orderly, neat, and efficient but nicely personal and warm. There was also a small lounge area with a dining table and a blue-covered banquette plus a wall mounted television set and medium-sized refrigerator. And again, there were some more photos of friends and family tacked up here and there.

They then went up a few steps and as they passed down a hall, Harding said, "I've saved the best for last." He led Kimber down a hallway which contained five staterooms, including one that he indicated was "Just for you." It was a handsome cabin with a large queen-sized bed covered in a rich white bedspread that was fitted to the bed. The room was beautifully paneled and had several oval-shaped windows that kept the room bright and airy. There were many built-in shelves, a small desk and chair, plus a comfortable armchair upholstered in white and blue fabric with a seashell motif that matched some throw pillows on the bed. Off to one side was a doorway that led to "The Head" or bathroom which consisted of a small, very efficient room with a sink, toilet with a built-in bidet, and a shower. "This is your stateroom. I hope you like it."

Kimber smiled warmly as she saw a bouquet of fresh peach-and-white peonies next to the sink. Looking at the bed, she mused, *I wonder if Harding is thinking of visiting me here some night and how do I feel about that? Well, we'll see...*

And then he said, "Just down this hall is my stateroom." He then led the way down the hall and opened a door onto a larger room with a king-sized bed, a *chaise longue*, a desk with a comfortable chair and many shelves filled with some books, but no photos, no real memorabilia… no sense of the owner, which Kimber found strange. No hint of his life and background. There was, however, a large closet lined in cedar filled with a wide selection of clothes and a sizeable head, which was larger than the one in the other cabin. Besides a shower, there was also a tub plus a counter with two sinks and a sizable medicine cabinet. All very luxurious, efficient, but again not very personal.

Later, Kimber discovered a laundry room that housed two washing machines, two dryers, plus an ironing area. There was also a small washing machine that was designated for any guests who wanted to do his or her own laundry. The boat clearly was carefully thought out, was handsome, efficient, and designed to be supportive to the whim of every guest. It also was clearly designed to take advantage of every square inch of its 134-foot length.

Having had the tour, Harding asked if Kimber would like someone to help her unpack, to which she shook her head and said that "It wouldn't be *nécessaire*." Harding consequently excused himself and left Kimber to unpack and get settled in.

That evening, by mutual agreement, they decided to meet on the stern to have cocktails and then, instead of going offshore to one of the many surrounding high-end restaurants, have a quiet dinner on board. It was as though both wanted a quiet, more intimate time to get to know one another better. *There's something about this man that makes me feel safe… protected*, Kimber thought to herself, and while there were no other guests yet, the presence of the crew gave her the comfort of not being isolated with a man she was yet to really know.

They had drinks on the rear deck to enjoy the setting sun, which was spectacular with its peach and lavender hues. It was almost like Harding had arranged it just for her and neither one could stop from smiling and enjoying this special time.

At one point Kimber said, "This is such a beautiful ship."

Harding replied with a bit of a teasing look in his eyes, "The difference between a ship and a boat is a boat can be carried by a ship to another location, but a ship cannot be carried by a boat."

To which Kimber said, "Well that's most confusing. Is this a boat or a ship?"

"We call this a yacht. Technically a yacht can be from 40

feet to 200 feet or more. I'm not sure at what point a yacht gets to be too large to be carried by a ship as I'm kinda new to this boat business," he said sheepishly.

Kimber found herself charmed by that little boy side to Harding, as she generally disliked men who were full of bravado and self-importance.

Later, Harding mentioned that as he was leaving Kimber's apartment in Paris, that he had noticed that there were an extraordinary number of locks on the front door. Maybe five. Being a less than subtle man, he said, "I saw that you had a rather large number of locks on your apartment door. What's that all about?"

To which Kimber said simply, "A woman alone can't be too careful," and left it at that. Harding thought, *I bet there's a story behind that, but I best not press her on this now. Maybe another time.*

After dinner, as they sat out on deck, Harding accidentally spilled his cup of coffee onto the deck and, while the cup didn't break, it made quite a mess.

Kimber reacted with an "Oh, *mon Dieu!*" and Harding quickly went into the galley to get some paper towels to clean things, up only to be told by Suzanne, one of the stewards, that she would take care of it. Harding started to say, "Don't bother, I made the mess, so I'll clean it up," when it became clear that it was the job of the help to clean up accidents and not the owner.

Kimber found this most interesting, as Harding was clearly not an elitist and was not above cleaning up any mess he might make. *I bet he's the same in business*, she thought.

Later, Harding asked if she'd like to go out for a walk, as he wanted this special day to go on and on, but Kimber said, "It's been a long day for me. Would you mind terribly if I retired early?"

To which Harding replied, "Of course not, I totally understand." He walked her down to her cabin and gave her a gentle kiss… soft and sweet, which was a relief to her as she was always on guard when it came to men and situations where she was somewhat defenseless.

Today had been very interesting and, in a way, exciting, as here was a man who, while being a bit rough around the edges, was considerate, caring, and not overly pushy or full of himself. All a relief considering this new adventure and the mysteries ahead. And so, she said, "Merci for the lovely day. I look forward to tomorrow," and gently closed the door, leaving him in the hallway grinning like a little boy. She waited a while to make sure he was gone and then quietly locked the door.

Earlier before dinner, she had unpacked. Suzanne had asked if she needed anything pressed or was there anything else *Mademoiselle* Lepelletier needed? To which Kimber thanked her and said, "*Non, merci.* I think everything is *trés bon.*"

And it was. There was ample closet space and the bathroom, or head as it was called, had every item one could possibly need, from a hair dryer to a small, zippered bag with toothpaste, nail file, and so forth. There was even a small sewing kit, which was rather redundant considering that anything like a loose button would clearly be taken care of by Suzanne or one of the other staff on hand. And so, Kimber brushed her teeth, creamed her face and body, gave her hair 200 strokes with the brush she had packed, wrote in her journal, and went to bed with a grin on her face. She had just had one of the best days for her in a long, long time.

Bright and early the next day, she met Harding in the salon. There was fresh coffee and an amazing assortment of pastries of but when Harding gestured towards them, Kimber politely refused and instead settled for a fresh croissant and a cup of black coffee. To Harding's surprise she dunked the croissant into the coffee with great delight.

"So, Captain, what the *plan de jour*?" Kimber asked with a somewhat wicked grin.

Harding looked a bit puzzled at first, but quickly figured out that she wanted to know what he had in mind for the day's activities. He replied, "Typically, I start the day with a workout as I have a lot of exercise equipment in my office, weights and such. Tommy, one of the guys who helps crew this boat, has a little side business as a trainer when he's on land and so he helps me stay motivated, as I by nature rather not exercise but know that it's a necessity and so I try to make it a part of my daily routine. You're free to join me if you'd like. Often, we move the weights out onto the deck which makes the whole routine more palatable."

Since both Harding and Kimber were in shorts and appropriate tops, they went to his office to gather up some weights, pads, and stretch bands, but they weren't there. "Ah, I bet Tommy has set them out on the deck already," and sure enough, when they reached the rear deck by the Jacuzzi, there was Tommy standing by a lineup of weights plus the stretch bands. The pads were already laid out on the deck, along with towels, bottles of ice-cold water, and Tommy, who sported a big grin.

"Ready to get your blood moving?" he asked in a cheery voice, so how could they refuse? He started the two of them off with some stretch exercises and then proceeded with various movements involving the weights, with him assigning Harding his usual weights and then giving somewhat lighter ones to Kimber.

The whole routine took maybe 40 minutes or so, and was surprisingly pleasant in that there was a considerable exchange of laughter and grins. Tommy had even set some fun disco music on the ship's speaker system, which gave a certain rhythm to the workout session. It was an extraordinarily beautiful day and how could one not enjoy this beginning of what Kimber hoped would be an extra special adventure? It certainly was an excellent start.

At the end of the session, Kimber thanked Tommy, and it was agreed that she would meet Harding on deck in an hour or so, the idea being that they would take a walk after he made some necessary business phone calls.

Kimber, meanwhile, wanted to relax with the book she had started on the plane. In any case, they would need to be back in time to meet his first guests, Ali and Lew Adelman.

Chapter Three
The First Arrivals

At 12:25 the white Rolls arrived with Ali and Lew Adelman. As a couple, they provided quite a contrast. Lew was a rather large, rotund man, a bit over six feet with broad shoulders, considerably overweight, with a flushed face and inclined to be on the disheveled side. He wore an expensive blue linen jacket with off-white cotton pants and with a yellow belt. His wardrobe proved to be a bad choice for traveling, as his clothes were now very wrinkled and gave one the impression that Lew was a slob and an inexperienced traveler, which was not necessarily the case. He simply tended to make bad choices with his wardrobe.

It turned out that Ali was always on his case "to clean up your act." She even, at one point, hired a wardrobe consultant while in Los Angeles to help him with his image, but that hardly made a dent in his disheveled appearance.

Ali, on the other hand, was petite and angular. She had a sharp face with a jutting nose and chin and tight lips that were accentuated by the bright lipstick she wore. While she gave a rather harsh impression facially, she had good instincts when it came to her wardrobe. She arrived wearing white slacks, a sea green and white print blouse with a matching green sweater carefully draped over her shoulders, and carried a green Gucci purse and shoes that matched the rest of her ensemble perfectly. She also sported a pair of sunglasses that looked incredibly expensive. In short, she was a very pulled-together woman and she knew it!

As they were getting out of the car, they were bickering in what they thought were low voices but in fact could easily be heard, and the discussion was about whether or not they should tip the driver. Harding, having left the yacht to greet them, heard their discussion and assured them that no tipping was necessary, and in fact while they were on board, tipping was strictly forbidden. Ali gave Lew one of those "I told you so" looks and walked ahead of him as Harding gestured for them to "Please come on board the 'Deeper and Deeper.'"

Once they were on board, Harding introduced them to Kimber as Tommy passed out glasses of champagne. When everyone had a glass, Harding raised his and said, "Welcome aboard. I hope you have an excellent time here with us and please, if you need anything, just ask any of the crew."

As they sipped their drinks, Harding led them past the open deck to the forward shaded area, where a table was set up for lunch with its blue china, blue napkins to match, and white tablecloth with blue piping. There were mahogany deck chairs on one side of the table and the seating on the other side was a blue-covered banquette seat, which was a good ten feet long. The supports for the roof were minimal, allowing for a spectacular view of the surrounding yachts. All very glamorous.

"Shall we have a bite of lunch while the crew takes your luggage down to your cabin, or would you rather get settled in first? Either way is fine with us, as we're having a cold lunch." Lew started to head for one of the dining chairs when he was stopped by Ali, who said, "I think we'd like to get settled in first if you don't mind." Whether she was saying this to Harding or to Lew was questionable.

"No problem," Harding replied. "Tommy here will show you to your cabin and when you get settled in, please come up and join us for lunch." And off they went, and one could hear them beginning to bicker again as they were led to their cabin.

When they were out of earshot, Kimber looked at Harding and asked, "Where on earth did you meet those two?"

"Oh, I've known Lew for some time. I met him while I was doing some work in Los Angeles. I barely know his wife, Ali. They're producers in the television field. Game shows, to be exact. They hit it big when they came up with a show called 'What Do You Know?' which stars Phil King. It's been on the air for five, maybe six years and has made them an incredible fortune. I'm not sure what Lew and Ali are really like. I met Lew some time ago and he intrigued me, so I invited them to join us. I hope it wasn't a mistake. Actually, I kind of hope to get them involved with a charity that I've been setting up to help kids who have become hooked on drugs. My aim is to get them clean and directed towards a productive life. I don't have kids of my own, so this is a way for me to do something with children that's constructive… something that will have a lasting effect. I don't know. My charity is in the early stages of getting set up. Ali and Lew don't have children, so maybe they might want to get involved. I sure hope so."

Tommy was soon up on deck and whispered into Harding's ear that there was a problem down below. Harding quickly excused himself and went down below to find the Adelmans having a heated discussion. The problem appeared to be the sleeping arrangements. Apparently, Lew tended to snore, and Ali did not like the idea of sharing the one large bed in their cabin with him. She wanted separate beds. Harding quickly suggested that they be moved to the cabin down the hall where there were two single beds and the Adelmans and their luggage were soon headed in that direction. Problem hopefully solved, at least for the moment.

Meanwhile, two more guests had arrived by train from Berlin and Mac had picked them up and brought them to the boat. Harding, having just settled the Adelmans into their revised accommodations, greeted the new guests with a smile and handshake. "Kimber, meet Natasha Dinara and…" At a loss for the name of the other guest, Natasha jumped in with "This is my very good friend, Frans Klamer." Everyone smiled, shook hands and talked over each other with a selection of "Hellos", "Glad to meet you," "How was your journey?" and so forth. Harding took the moment to say, "For those who are not in the know, Natasha here is a remarkable ballet dancer…. a world famous one." He said this proudly, as if he had accomplished something extraordinary in securing her as a guest. Natasha brushed off the compliment but was clearly pleased with the recognition.

Meanwhile, Mac had carried their luggage up on deck and proceeded to give Tommy a hand lugging it below, with instructions from Harding to put them in the cabin that had originally been assigned to the Adelmans. As this was going on, Harding pulled Natasha aside and explained that there had been a problem and that the cabin originally assigned to them had been taken by another couple, and would it be ok if Natasha and Frans had to share a bed, to which Natasha said with a big smile and a hint of a Russian accent "Absolutely no problem. It's an arrangement that we're very familiar with."

And so, Harding showed them to their cabin and, after a quick look around, they came back up on deck just as Suzanne finished arranging two more place settings at the table. They were soon joined by Ali and Lew, who were having a disagreement over who should have packed the sunscreen, to which Harding said, "No problem. You'll find plenty of that in your stateroom head. Now, let's all have an enjoyable lunch." The latter came out sounding more like "Let's not have any more negativity."

Within moments, Suzanne, with the help of Claude, served a delicious cold salad of lobster and shrimp, to everyone's delight. However, Harding noticed that Ali was pushing the shrimp to one side. He asked, "Is there something wrong with the salad, Ali?"

"Oh, I can't eat shrimp." Her face, which had naturally sharp features, took on a sour, disgusted expression. "I have a major problem with them... I break out and have great difficulty breathing. There was one time when there was shrimp in a salad I had on my first-class flight from New York to L.A. and my reaction was so severe they had to make an emergency landing and I almost died! I couldn't breathe. In fact, if you don't mind, I would like something else as even the slightest taste of shrimp will make me deathly ill."

Harding, not wanting her to have any problems, was about to ask Suzanne to replace Ali's salad, but Suzanne had already started to clear her place. "Would you like a nice fruit salad or maybe some cold cuts?" Suzanne asked, to which Ali said in rather a disappointed voice, "Oh, I suppose a salad will do but what kind of dressing is available? I really only like balsamic vinegar."

"No problem," Suzanne replied, although it was clear that it was a considerable imposition which Ali either didn't pick up on or chose to ignore. However, Harding noticed that Suzanne gave Ali a rather strange once over… a curious look of interest that didn't make sense.

"How was your journey?" Kimber asked Lew to get off the shrimp subject, but before he could answer, Ali jumped in with "It was a nightmare. We started the trip with a flight from LA to London where we saw a few shows that we were interested in financing when they come to New York. It helped break up that long flight from LA to here. Unfortunately, the three shows we saw were a disaster. Two were just so boring. I wanted to walk out during the intermissions and the third we liked but found out that it already had producers set for the New York run so London was a total fiasco... A waste of our time," she said with disgust. "However, we were able to meet with the London producers who bought the rights to our show 'What Do You Know?' I'm sure you've heard of it, and so the trip to London wasn't a total waste. Close, but not a total disaster and of course we can write off this trip for tax purposes."

To change the subject, Harding suddenly suggested that everyone get settled in then, after drinks and dinner this evening, "We'll all go to the Casino."

"Now that's a marvelous idea," said Kimber. "I was hoping someone would suggest it, as going to the Casino used to be such fun. When I was younger, much younger, I was in love with a marvelous man named René who used to take me there. In those days everyone dressed. The men in tuxedos, the women in gowns. Oh, the clothes we women wore! All so *trés elégante*! I suspect it won't be as special now, but we can go all dressed up and add a special *savoir-faire* to the evening, no?"

Ali said, "I'm all up for it." At the same time Lew said, "Oh I'm not really in the mood to get into one of those damned monkey suits," but Ali quickly said, "Listen, you knew we were going to go to some dress-up places… besides, I'm dying to gamble a bit, so just be quiet."

Natasha chimed in, "Oh, let's do it. It should be such fun. It's been ages since I've gone to a casino." But then a slight cloud passed over her beautiful face as if she were having second thoughts.

Harding said, "Then it's a done deal. Hopefully, our last two guests, Jenny and Ron Ward, will have arrived in time. Meanwhile, I suggest that everyone get settled in, relax, sun, use the Jacuzzi, take a nap, whatever. If you need anything, just ask Claude or Suzanne. We'll plan to eat around eight o'clock, so why don't you all meet up here for drinks at 7 and be formally dressed to go on to the Casino after dinner."

All nodded their heads in agreement and headed off. Lew was heard to mutter to Ali "Are you sure I have to get into that damned tux?" to which Ali said with more than a little irritation, "Well, yeah. And don't forget to bring your wallet as I intend to do some gambling."

There were some indecipherable mutterings from Lew as they went down to their cabin. Meanwhile, Natasha was heard to say to Frans, "How about our taking a nap and then maybe lounge around, use the Jacuzzi or whatever?" Frans was heard to say "Hmmmm, love our 'whatevers!'" and gave her a pat on her backside as they went down the steps.

Harding grinned happily and said to Kimber, "How about we move over onto two of those chaises?"

To which Kimber gently suggested, "If you don't mind, could we use those two over there that are out of the sun?" She walked over to one of them, took off a sort of robe she had been wearing to reveal that she had on a very elegant one-piece bathing suit that showed that age had not robbed her of her looks. She then promptly took a tube of sunscreen out of a large bag and proceeded to apply a layer on her face, arms, and legs. When she was done, she gestured toward Harding, asking, "Would you mind doing my back, *s'il vous plaît?*"

Harding gladly obliged and when he was finished, he quickly said, "I'll be right back." He raced down to his cabin and returned, having quickly changed into a black Speedo that showed that his workouts with Tommy were clearly paying off. Harding lost no time in asking Kimber to put some sunscreen on his muscular back, although it was clear he was one of those people who is able to tan easily and spent a good amount of time in the sun. Kimber took one look at Harding's deep tan, shrugged, grinned, and started smoothing the cream over his back. It was hard to tell who was enjoying the application the most.

And so, the two of them spent a leisurely afternoon relaxing and enjoying the shared time together. The sweet sea breeze was soothing and relaxing. Someone far off was playing some soft jazz music. The day could not have been more agreeable!

The only interruption was a call from Ron Ward saying that he and his wife Jenny were running late but would arrive around 5:00. It was agreed that the timing was perfectly okay in that it would still give the Wards time to settle in, get dressed for the evening and join the rest for drinks at 7:00.

A bit later there was another interruption when Harding discovered a series of towels engraved with his initials in his stateroom. When he asked Claude about them, Claude, as the head steward, replied that the towels in Harding's cabin were starting to show their age and he decided to replace them. This did not sit well with Harding as, first: he strongly disliked the idea of monogrammed towels, and second: he preferred to be the one making those decisions. He was not about to have someone else making them.

As tactfully as he could, he said, "I appreciate the care you put into keeping the 'Deeper and Deeper' in top shape, but in the future please consult me on such decisions. I normally don't care about the cost of such small items, but I do have a strong dislike for initialed items, as they reek of elitism and ego aggrandizement." It was not clear that Claude understood the nuance of the issue, but he got the message. Interestingly enough, the yacht came with some very expensive, tasteful China and crystal which Harding was in the process of learning to appreciate. He was a work in progress.

Chapter Four
Drinks, Dinner, and Diversion

At 7:00 the group gathered in the grand salon with its warm pearwood paneling, pale grey wall-to-wall carpeting and upholstered furniture to match. All were in formal wear as requested. The Wards, Ron and Jenny, were introduced, as many of the guests had not been on deck when they arrived. At the far end there was a long sofa that could easily seat six which went along one wall and curved inwards as if to embrace any arriving guests. There were also numerous large comfortable armchairs. In one corner there was a game table with six chairs and in the other was a white baby grand piano.

Drinks orders were quickly taken by Claude and Suzanne, and were soon passed around along with hors d'oeuvres. Everyone looked stunning: the men were in tuxedos and the ladies looked particularly glamorous: Ali in a sea-green long gown with shoes and purse which matched her gown perfectly and a necklace and bracelet in jade and diamonds to compete her look. While she might be disagreeable at times, the lady certainly had a wonderful sense of style.

Jenny Ward was in a burgundy cocktail length dress which, while not as elegant as Ali's, still made her look attractive. Ali was heard to say when she saw Jenny's outfit, "Very nice," as her voice dripped with insincerity. Jenny tried to ignore her comment, but Ron bristled at the subtle insult. Ali was also heard to say about Jenny's necklace that "it certainly was odd." Overhearing this, Ron said, rather coolly, "I gave Jenny that necklace. It's made from carved olive wood which is inset with tiny cola-colored diamonds made to look like a relic unearthed from a Celtic burial ground."

Later, he confided to Harding that when he found out that Jenny loved the piece he had splurged and bought it for her at auction at Christies London for $13,000. He went on to say that one made from wood and brown diamonds sold at Sotheby's in February for $103,000.

As for Natasha's beige outfit, while it had not cost a great deal, on Natasha, because of her superb posture, it looked remarkable. She simply demanded attention and she clearly knew how to be a star... she radiated glamour.

But maybe, because of her European background, Kimber had it over all the other women when it came to having great style. She was in a beautiful yellow chiffon gown that had a simple but elegant drape to it which accentuated her fine figure. Her jewelry consisted of a gold-like beaded necklace with earrings and bracelets to match. Harding took one look and thought, *Oh my God, how I wish she were all mine. She has more style than anyone else onboard.*

A while later everyone turned to see Harding seated at the baby grand as he started to play "Isn't It Romantic?" But he modified the words and sang in a modest voice, "Isn't she romantic?" as he looked around the room but ended up setting his look on Kimber.

Everyone came over, drink in hand, to gather around the piano, only to discover that his hands weren't really pressing down the keys. The keys were moving on their own and the sound was coming from a player piano! There was much laughter, and Natasha and Frans started to dance. The yacht gently rocked, and it was a charming moment and certainly romantic for some of the guests.

At 8:00 promptly, Claude announced that dinner was served, and everyone put down his or her drinks and moved to the inner salon with its dining table. Harding held out a chair at one end of the table and gestured for Kimber to sit in it and then sat at the other end while the others took the remaining seats. The table was set with a crisp white linen tablecloth, blue and white Copenhagen china in the half lace pattern; the silver was George Jensen's acorn pattern and the Waterford water and wine glasses were in the Lismore pattern. In the center was a large silver Revere bowl filled with white peonies and orchids. Harding set the piano to play soft background music in the style of Beegie Adair and everyone settled in to have a fine dinner.

Claude and Suzanne, who was Claude's assistant and common-law partner, quickly poured the wine, a selection of Sancerre Cottat from the Loire Valley for the white and Wolf Blass Red Label Shiraz Cabernet for the red. When everyone had his glass filled, Harding proposed a toast, his eyes scanning the table. "I want to welcome everyone here on 'Deeper and Deeper.'" With a sly smile, he added, looking at Kimber, "I hope you have a remarkable time here and that it leads to many more wonderful adventures," to which there were many echoes of "Cheers", "Salute" and even one "Bottoms up!"

Prior to dinner, Claude had asked the various guests what their preference was: meat or fish, with Ali requesting a vegetarian dish. The conversation around the table was lively with the subjects ranging from politics to gossip about several celebrities. At one point, Ali turned to Ron and said, "I hear that you're a doctor. May I ask what's your specialty?"

Ron casually said, "I'm a neurosurgeon."

"What's a neurosurgeon?" asked Natasha. "I know it's a medical title of sorts, but what does it cover? What do you specialize in?"

Kimber noticed that Harding looked a little nervous and wondered, *What's that about?*

Ron simply said, "I operate on the brain." Suddenly the table got very silent as he now had the full attention of everyone. Few, if any, had ever met a neurosurgeon.

"The brain!" said Ali. "How fascinating! I realize I'm asking a complicated question, but what does your work consist of?"

Ron thought for a moment, then said, "I realize most people have no idea of what my work entails. A short description would be that it consists of cutting into the stuff that creates thought, feeling, and reason. It is an amazing field in that when all goes well, one often manages to save a person's life, often to make that life richer or at least manageable. The problem occurs when the work doesn't go right. The consequences can be devastating and often can result in death. It can be devastating not only for the patient but for the doctor. For example: When operating with the intent to remove a tumor, knowing that unless it's removed, the patient will surely die. Then once I'm into the brain I find that it is impossible to safely remove all of the tumor, I have to deal with the knowledge that the patient might gain some additional time to live but the poor guy has basically a death sentence and there is nothing I can do except stall the inevitable."

"The worst part of the job is that sometimes in the process of operating, some part of the brain is accidentally cut, with the result that the patient is crippled or dies. The sad part is there is no way to become a really fine surgeon without making mistakes in one's early years of operating. I'm a highly experienced surgeon and, as a consequence, a very good surgeon, but the price that others have had to pay for me to learn my trade is devastating and something I have to live with every day of my life. The fact is that every time I operate, there is the chance that I might damage or kill the patient and that is a terrible position to be in. However, if I don't operate, the patient will surely die or suffer incredibly."

"Being here on this boat is so wonderful as it's an escape from the world of disease and death in which I spend much of my life. When one saves a life, it's thrilling. However, it is very difficult when one has to tell a patient that I cannot save him, especially if I'm dealing with a young child with distressed parents. The problem is made even greater if I'm not entirely certain I'm right. It is easy to deal with patients who will certainly die, but torture for me when it's not clear how to save the patient or if one can actually cure the problem."

This last statement was met with silence except for the soft background sound of Beegie Adair playing "Where or When."

Kimber noted that Harding had become very quiet. but, not knowing the cause, she was helpless to know how to be supportive. Meanwhile, Claude and Suzanne cleared the main course and brought out a beautiful bombe with a meringue topping. Suzanne presented it to Harding, who looked at it with a sly look of confusion as to what to do after trying to cut through the meringue and finding it too hard to penetrate in spite of the fact that he had a very large, sharp knife!

Suddenly, Kimber chimed in with "Give it here. I know exactly what to do." And after Suzanne picked it up and carried it over to Kimber and placed it in front of her, Kimber raised the knife and with one swift, rather violent swing of the knife, she cut cleanly through the rigid meringue amid a volley of laughter and applause, to which Kimber said to Suzanne, "I suggest you take it into the galley and cut it up there."

Shortly, pieces of the bombe were distributed by Suzanne and Claude along with a fine Veuve Clicquot champagne, and the guests settled into a quiet discussion of Natasha's latest triumph and the fact that her partner in one of the duets had "gone up." That's when a dancer totally forgets the next dance steps. Natasha explained, along with illustrating the steps involved, that she had to improvise around the poor guy until he remembered his moves again, which, thankfully had only been a matter of moments and was not noticed by the various dance reviewers in attendance. *"Quelle horrible!"* exclaimed Kimber to everyone's delight.

Later as Claude and Suzanne were clearing the table, Claude was heard to say "I saw you having words with Ali. What was that all about?"

Suzanne replied in a dismissive tone, "Oh, it was nothing." Lew overheard her and wondered if Ali had once again alienated someone, Suzanne in particular. He wished he had the guts to confront Ali about this pattern that lately seemed to crop up more and more at regular intervals in their lives.

It was then that Harding produced a silver tray on which there were eight long white envelopes. He proceeded to say "Please, everyone take an envelope and don't open it until you get to the Casino." Everyone proceeded to take an envelope with a range of curiosity registered on each of their faces. Harding had an additional driver waiting with a second white Rolls Royce and the party left the boat and headed for the Casino De Monte Carlo amid much talk and laughter.

The two cars drove up to the front door of the casino and as the guests were getting out of the cars, Mac, who had chaffered the lead car, rushed ahead and paid the 18 Euros admission for each guest. Harding then led the group into the casino with its huge glass domed ceiling accented by eight large crystal chandeliers that hovered above the gaming tables. Built in 1863 as a pioneer of the Belle Epoque era, the room was dazzling. While everyone in Harding's party was in formal attire, most of the other patrons were either in formal clothing or, at the very least, the gentlemen were dressed in black business suits with ties and dark shoes and the women were in gowns or cocktail dresses with some in pantsuits. Lew was seen to nudge Ali as he gestured towards the gentlemen in dark business suits as if to say, "See, I could have avoided wearing this fucking tux!"

Harding arranged for everyone to first have a drink and then announced over the unique sounds of the roulette wheels, cheers of the winners, and occasional groans of the less fortunate, "Please, everyone open your envelope and have a fun time!" What each person found was a small stack of Euros equating to about $1,000. This was greeted with a wide variety of reactions: Natasha was delighted, and Frans was a bit overwhelmed. Ali and Lew seemed pleased and acted as if it was nothing out of the ordinary. Ron and Jenny were a bit surprised and a bit taken aback, but it was Kimber's reaction that interested Harding the most. And it was not what he expected. She was clearly annoyed, not at all pleased, and said not a word... No "Thank you," no "What a fun idea"… nothing!

And so, everyone spread out and hit the tables. That is, all except Kimber, who was last seen walking out on the terrace away from the gaming. It was later when Harding finally cornered her and asked her, "What's wrong? What did I do that's so terrible?"

Kimber took a deep breath and then said, "What were you thinking? Do you realize that throwing money around like that is vulgar and in the worst of taste? First of all, think how this will affect Natasha and Frans. Whether you realize it or not, Natasha obviously needs to live carefully as her big earning days are clearly over, and she will surely lose the money tonight for no other reason than to amuse you. As for Frans, I'm sure he'll lose his money as well, and it will be very frustrating for him. That is, unless he's smart enough and pockets as much as he thinks he can get away with. My bet is that he would do anything to just hold onto that money but no, to amuse you he will have to gamble it away. Or at least appear to gamble it all away."

"Ron and Jenny obviously have considerable wealth and this gesture of yours is just a nouveau riche man showing off. As for Ali and Lew, I suspect you found company there as, from what I can tell, they live and breathe money and little else. Earlier, they bent my ear bragging about their palatial home in Beverly Hills and the money their television game show brings in. It's a sad joke that the man they hired as their English butler quit working for them because they never entertain. It seems that they have very few friends. So, your little gesture resonated with them. I'm sorry, Harding, but what you did was vulgar and thought-less." And with that she handed him her envelope, turned around and continued to walk around the balcony, leaving Harding alone and devastated.

Chapter Five
Who Do You Think I Am?

The next day was very low-key. Lew had what looked like a colossal hangover and Ali had mysteriously disappeared, God knows where. Natasha and Frans were frustrated and sad, having lost the money that they both could have used, although Frans was indeed able to pocket a small portion of the cash. The Wards had gone for a walk early that morning, as Ron was used to going to work in the early hours and his body didn't register that he was on vacation. But it was Kimber who was the surprise.

She acted as though nothing had transpired the night before. She was her usual cheery self and pushed for Harding to join her in exercising out on the deck after breakfast.

Harding was relieved but confused by this and, because he had an inquisitive mind and very much wanted this budding relationship to work, he finally blurted out. "Listen, I'm sorry I was such an ass. I just wanted everyone to have a good time and it was a gesture that I could easily afford. You made it perfectly clear that it was a bad idea… a really BAD idea. So can you accept my apology, and can we leave this behind us?"

"But of course," she said patting him on his cheek. "Lesson learned… I hope."

And so, they worked out on the deck with Tommy and they concentrated on enjoying the day and each other's company. At one point, Harding said, "With the exception of the idea of going to the Casino, I really have no other plans in mind as to how to entertain everyone. Any thoughts?"

"Hmmm," muttered Kimber. "A while ago my friend Fleur, who is great fun, told me about a party that she had gone to where the guests were asked to come dressed as their favorite movie star. Apparently, there were some amazing results, both good and bad." She said with kind of a wicked smile "How about if we put together a similar party but stipulate that everyone has to improvise his or her costume. That is no one is allowed to go to a costume rental shop for a professional costume."

Harding thought for a brief second and replied enthusiastically, "I love it… What a fun idea! Great, now you'll have me cornered and will see how inventive I can be… or not!"

That afternoon, with some creative input from Olivier, who besides being the first mate, had a background in computers, Harding and Kimber designed an eye-catching announcement that invited the recipient to attend a "Costume Party" to be held on the "Deeper and Deeper" in four nights' time starting at 9:00 PM. The one requirement for admission was one had to be dressed in an improvised costume that represented one's favorite movie star in his or her most famous role… absolutely no rental costumes. The rule was no costume = no admission. Prizes would be awarded for the most original and the funniest costume. Tommy and Mac were assigned the job of getting the invitations printed up and distributed to the folks around the Yacht Club. Word quickly spread and despite the short notice, there were lots of R.S.V.P.'s the next day.

With that, everyone went to work on decorating the yacht as well as creating their costume. Harding was confused and amused when Kimber asked him if she could have a pair of his long black socks to dress up her costume. She made it clear that he would not want them back when she was through with them. Harding himself went crazy looking for a prop he needed for his costume and ended securing a coil of heavy electric wire and some black electric tape from Watson, the ship's engineer. Part of his costume required a prop pistol, so Harding went to his safe and removed a handgun he stored there and carefully removed all the bullets.

Harding and Kimber drove themselves wild trying to come up with special prizes for the most ingenious and the most amusing costume or costumes. They finally settled on gift certificates for dinner for two at the *Hôtel de Paris*. Not inspired, but it solved the problem.

During the time everyone was busy helping to set up the party, Natasha and Frans were mostly absent. They had Mac drive them to a special place and had him swear that he would not tell anyone what they were up to. For these clandestine trips they seemed to be in gym clothing, although Natasha carried a rather large skirt with her, and Frans carried a portable Bluetooth speaker. They seemed to always return very excited and bursting with smiles.

As for decorations: at the suggestion of Tommy, Harding called up a woman named Colette and after explaining the party plan, they asked if she was free to lend a hand in pulling the party together. Colette seemed very agreeable to the idea and mentioned that she had been involved in a number of parties thrown at the *Hôtel de Paris* as well as theatrical events staged at the *Salle Garnier Monte Carlo*.

She sounded perfect for the job and agreed to come to the yacht at 2:00 PM.

She arrived promptly and managed to startle everyone with her appearance. She had long bright orange and yellow dyed hair, tattoos over 40 or more percent of her body, including her face and neck as well sporting numerous piercings around her mouth and ears. At first she was a bit off-putting, but it soon became clear that she was extremely smart and clever… all the things they wanted the party to be. The first thing she suggested was that she would bring some books that she had at home on Hollywood and famous people so that they could have the photos blown up and mounted on Foam Core and simply framed. As The photos would be very lightweight, so they could easily replace the existing artwork in the main salon and other public areas of the yacht.

Among the blowups would be images of Marlon Brando in *The Wild One*, Gloria Swanson in *Sunset Boulevard*, Marilyn Monroe in *Gentlemen Prefer Blondes*, Cary Grant in *North by Northwest*, Joan Crawford and Bette Davis in *Whatever Happened to Baby Jane?*, Frank Sinatra and Sammy Davis Jr. in *Ocean's Eleven*, Mae West in *She Done Him Wrong*, and one of Vivien Leigh, Clark Gable, and Hattie McDaniel in *Gone With the Wind*.

It posed a problem finding black stars from old films and, hopefully, the few they found would satisfy everyone, as both Harding and Kimber were liberals and socially aware. Colette also directed them to a local party store that carried a wide selection of balloons that could be helium-filled. and suggested that they get three grosses of large balloons in the shape of stars that ranged in colors from white to clear to gold and silver.

The larger balloons could even have small electric battery powered lights inside them... all very theatrical. Kimber suggested that they rent a red carpet for in front of the yacht and hired a cameraman plus a man in a white tuxedo with a microphone to "interview" the arrivals. Colette suggested that they hire a man she knew from the local television studio. The interviews would be broadcast over a tv setup at various strategic areas of the yacht, plus at the nearby Yacht Club's bar, adding additional cachet to the evening. Using this man guaranteed that there would be some local TV coverage of the party making the event even bigger.

Ali finally got in the party mood and suggested that they should have klieg lights "like they do for the real Oscars," and Philip, the yacht's captain, came up with a source for renting three of the lights which would be set up on the dock to shoot shafts of light into the sky like a Hollywood premiere. Colette helped find a location that would rent period costumes for the crew as well as another source that could provide a ton of food ranging from caviar to *petit fours* in the shape of stars.

Harding had wanted to get two large Academy Awards statues for the party, but soon learned that the Oscar image was trademarked and such statues were not readily available, so he settled on having Colette get two ten-foot-tall blowups made of the Academy Award statue. These proved to be too tall for inside the yacht and ended up being delegated to the outside entrance and looked amazingly impressive. When guests were photographed in front of these cutouts, the photos looked like the guest was standing in front of real three-dimensional Oscars.

The only negative came from Ali, who was overheard to say to Colette with reference to her tattoos, "What a stupid thing to do to your body. What a foolish—and I'll say it again—stupid girl you are!" While she went on saying how appalled she was by all the tattoos, strangely, she made no comments about the piercings. To Colette's credit, she tried to ignore Ali's remarks, but one could tell that she was upset and really very angry at Ali and her thoughtless diatribe. The fact that she didn't vocally retaliate proved that Colette had more class and style than Ali.

And so, everyone pitched in to make this event "really terrific." The day of the party, Kimber counted the RSVP's and there were well over five dozen acceptances. It appeared that the entire Yacht Club was going to show up, so the food and drink order was increased, and Colette hired a security company to control the situation should the need arise.

It was during this time that Ali ran into Suzanne while the latter was doing some work in the laundry room. "So, tell me, are you swamped with the preparation for the party?" asked Ali.

"Not really," she replied. "When Mr. Leith was the ship's original owner, we had many large parties, and they were great fun. So many interesting people. Especially some of the ladies."

"How so?" asked Ali.

"Well, you know, some of those ladies from New York could be great fun."

"Mmmm. Is that true?" asked Ali, who extended her hand to brush against Suzanne's.

"Oh, you know, they're, how should I say… maybe a bit more sophisticated, more worldly." With that, Suzanne took hold of Ali's hand. When Ali didn't pull back, Suzanne smiled and gently touched her face.

"Ah, I see what you mean," Ali said. "What an interesting woman you are. I'd like to get to know you better."

"Well, we might just do that, as I suspect you and I have more in common than anyone might suspect." Suzanne said, smiling. This was followed by Ali's hand drifting over Suzanne's face and moving slowly down and ending on her breast. When there was no resistance, Ali moved even closer and slowly gave her a kiss, a kiss that was gentle at first and again, when there was no resistance, the kiss became more and more passionate.

Suzanne pulled back, went to the door, closed it, and, pressing her back to it, said, "Get over here."

Ali walked over to her and, with a smirk on her face, said, "Are you sure you're up to this?" and kissed her with a fierce desire that was matched in full by Suzanne.

After some moments of wild sexual abandonment, Suzanne pulled back and said, "This is too dangerous. Meet me here when everyone has gone to bed and let's really connect." Ali grinned happily and said, "See you then. Shall we say 11:30 tonight here?"

Both women nodded in agreement and Ali left quickly and Suzanne waited a bit and then wandered out.

Later that night, both women slipped out of their respective cabins when their husbands were asleep and met again in the laundry room. Suzanne said, "You have no idea how long it's been for me to have some really good sex." She grabbed Ali's robe and pulled it violently open and attacked her. While Ali was excited about the aggressiveness of the move, Suzanne started roughly grabbing and then biting Ali's breasts.

What was at first exciting soon became more of a battle between that of the aggressor and that of the prey, and Ali didn't like it one bit. She yearned for some tender attention, something that was obviously missing in her marriage. But this was way too violent and harsh. She was afraid to yell out and inadvertently alert others on the boat but how could she protect herself? She said in a low harsh voice, "Stop it! You're hurting me."

Suzanne said, "Oh don't give me that shit. You love it."

"No. I don't! I'm leaving… I'll have you fired!"

Suzanne grabbed her, preventing her from leaving and snarled, "There's no fucking way you'll do that. Just try it and I'll fill Lew's ears with words that'll make his head spin. I don't think you want a divorce now, do you? Go back to your cozy little cabin and your fat husband and think about it. Just know that I'm not through with you!"

Suzanne pushed Ali into a nearby washing machine, which made a loud crashing noise, and stormed out of the door. She didn't realize that Lew had awakened and, seeing that Ali was gone, was looking for her to see if she was okay. As he was coming down an outer hall, he overheard Suzanne and Ali and the last part of their confrontation, and hid in an alcove until Suzanne had stormed out, then went up to the upper deck to fume.

Ali, who was left breathing hard, tried to pull herself together before leaving the laundry room. She had a hard time calming down, which was essential if she was to return to her cabin and not let Lew find out what had happened—that is, if he was awake. Lew quickly went to his cabin, got into his bed, and pretended to be asleep when Ali sneaked back in and got into her bed.

While there was no further noise, there was a notable tension in the air in contrast to the gentle rocking of the "Deeper and Deeper," whose very name seemed to mock certain of its occupants and where their relationships were going.

The next day, there was a strange moment when Claude and Suzanne were overheard to be having words while working in the galley. Claude, usually the epitome of decorum, was heard to call Suzanne "*Une clochard*" or tramp. On hearing this, Suzanne took a half-empty glass of wine from the counter, and flung the contents at Claude, and stormed off, leaving him to wipe the wine off and try to act as though nothing had happened. Claude must have overheard some of the interaction between Suzanne and Ali and was badly shaken by what he suspected. Consequently, he went down to their cabin to mull things over and, hopefully, recover some composure.

Meanwhile, Lew was seen to be upset as well and was having a hard time getting some ice for his glass of white wine. He picked up an ice pick and attacked one of the ice buckets, savagely stabbing at the ice over and over, to everyone's amazement and curiosity. *Where was that frustration and hostility coming from?* Harding wondered.

As for the party preparations, besides the Hollywood decor, Harding and Kimber had arranged to have most of the deck furniture plus the two Wave Runners picked up and stored off the boat so that there would be plenty of room to dance. A small band was hired and was positioned in the helm station in view of the dance floor but out of the way. Colette issued each member a gold sequined bowtie and hat to wear with their white dinner jackets.

Captain Molina had all the cabin doors locked as a control factor, as there would be a lot of strangers wandering about the yacht during the party. The doors to the laundry and engine rooms didn't have locks, so they remained unlocked. *But what did that matter? They both were of no importance to the party's functions*, he thought.

Even before 9:00 PM, people started to show up. The security team stood at the entrance and made sure everyone who showed up was in costume and had an invitation. There were several folks, who seeing the Klieg lights, were attracted to the boat, but without an invitation were politely turned away. Those who were in costumes and on the invitation list were directed up the red carpet to the "Photo Shoot" area, where they were interviewed and their picture and their names plus their addresses were taken so that the 8x10 photos of them could be delivered by hand the next day.

As the guests boarded the yacht, two men in tuxedos

and gold sequin-covered top hats carried trays of drinks and offered champagne, white or red wine, or a non-alcoholic beverage to guests. If someone wanted something else, they were directed towards the bar, where two hired bartenders in similar attire took orders. Three waitresses who were dressed as Busby Berkeley dancers with short gold-sequined outfits, mesh hose studded with rhinestones, blonde wigs, and big smiles passed out *hors d'oeuvres.*

The costume theme turned out to be the big hit of the party, as everyone got into the fun of it. Harding looked wonderfully virile with a well-worn cowboy hat and torn white shirt with appropriate stains that was opened to expose his muscular chest. He carried a make-believe whip made of the coiled electric wire and tape and to complete the image he had a real revolver... the perfect Indiana Jones.

"Is that gun real?" Kimber asked, looking concerned.

"Sure," he replied. I had it in my safe. Do you have a problem with that?"

"Well... yes, I hate guns and all they represent."

When Harding looked doubtful, Kimber said sternly, "I mean it! "

"OK, I get it, but I assure you that it has no bullets " With that he made a mock show of shooting at one of the photos of John Wayne. "Bam, bam!" he yelled as he made a token motion of shooting Wayne.

"Do me a favor, Harding, after the party, please put that

gun away. I never want to see it again. Do you hear me?"

Harding smiled in return, saluted her and said in a mocking tone, "As you wish, Madame." He thought to himself, *I'll keep it in my office as she never goes in there.*

Colette had shown up early, way before the guests were to arrive, and at first no one recognized her. She wore a floor-length ice blue gown with long gloves to match, which covered most of her tattoos. She had dyed her hair a pale gold and wore it in a large braid that ran down her back. The tattoos around her face and neck, which would normally have shown, were covered with an ice blue makeup and she had removed most of her piercings to create an astounding image of Elsa, the Snow Queen from *Frozen*. She was remarkably beautiful and, strangely, her personality changed with her appearance. Instead of being her usual warm and charming self, Colette now became cool and remote, almost scary.

Harding was a bit thrown by this new dimension to this fascinating lady. At a quiet moment before the guests were to arrive, he found her in a corner of the salon and, after some idle talk, he steered the conversation in a direction where he could ask her some questions about her past and what had led her to have the excessive number of tattoos and piercings.

To Harding's delight, Colette was quite open to talking about herself. She explained that she graduated from high school in 2006 with first honors and had never missed a day of class. She had first wanted to go to cosmetology school, but her mother put a lot of pressure on her to choose something else. What Colette really wanted to do was to go to a school to study forensic science, but her mother put a damper on that idea as well, telling Colette that she would have to become a police officer first. Her mother claimed that she had called the local police station and was told that bit of information. It turned out this was a lie.

Now, in her 30's, Colette was unable to pursue her dream without enough money to live away from home, go full-time to school, and work a job to pay for everything. Harding mused about financing the education she dreamed of.

When Harding asked about the many tattoos that seemed to cover about 40% of her body, Colette said, "I love collecting art and now I am art!" She went on to say, "My mother took me to get my first tattoo when I was 16 years old. Mom prefers small tattoos that can be hidden, but what's the fun of that?" Harding wondered if getting all those tattoos was her way of getting back at her mother. It would be easy to dismiss Colette as foolish, but she was obviously very intelligent, and it bothered him that she might be missing out on having a productive life. This was something that saddened him.

Realizing this, he ventured to say, "Your character is so

interesting. She's a character who must face her inner demons and thaw out her inner frosty aloofness and embrace life. It's of course none of my business, but I wonder if you dressed up as this character because she represents kind of a repressed and isolated part of yourself. Maybe you could, like your character, take charge of all that life can deal out and let go of any fear that's there. I could be way off base but your choice of character is fascinating as are you."

Colette smiled and said, "That's very perceptive of you, Harding," and went off to check on something on the upper deck.

Ali and Lew showed up as Laurel and Hardy, as they had bodies that somewhat matched that famous duo. Lew's rotund body mimicked Hardy's and Ali's slight, angular frame made a believable Laurel. Both had black hats and Lew got some electrical tape from the crew and made a short moustache a la Hardy's.

Natasha and Frans topped them by showing up as Fred Astaire and Ginger Rogers, as she had the perfect white flowing gown trimmed with feathers and wore her blonde hair in the Ginger Rogers style. She had spent the afternoon taking a feathered stole apart and sewing the feathers onto the edge of a white gown she had brought along for the trip. Frans, who had packed a black tux, was able to add a boutonniere and a red sash across his chest "to dress things up a bit" in honor of Fred Astaire.

Jenny and Ron came as characters from *One Flew Over the Cuckoo's Nest*, she as Nurse Ratchet in a starched white uniform, which had been a white summer dress which she altered. She styled her hair like her character, swept back with its center part topped by a nurse's cap made from some white cardboard she had found at a nearby art store. She also filled out her bosom like the character in the movie.

As Jack Nicholson's character, Ron wore faded Levis, an olive crew neck shirt coved by a Chambray shirt, a watch cap, and heavy work boots. But the hit part of his costume was an item Jenny made from several pillowcases—a straitjacket with a fake arm tied across his chest but with his one good arm conveniently free to hold a drink. There was some discussion whether Nicholson's character had ever appeared in a straitjacket, but everyone loved the image.

The only problem was that while the characters Jenny and Ron portrayed were supposedly antagonistic towards each other, Jenny and Ron were still so in love with each other that it was impossible for them to act as though they were adversaries. It was strange for the guests to see these hostile characters dancing affectionately with each other.

Kimber's costume was a big hit. She had shown up in a long black evening gown which she had luckily packed and was wearing black high-heeled shoes. Her hair was piled high on her head with a large costume diamond brooch pinned to the center of it, and she wore her travel necklace around her long, elegant neck. She had improvised a stretched-out cigarette holder and Harding's long black socks, cut open at the toe ends, made for long evening gloves and helped to create the perfect *Breakfast at Tiffany's* image of Audrey Hepburn as Holly Golightly. She looked dazzling! Harding had a hard time keeping his eyes off her.

The whole evening was highly successful and ended up being great fun with everyone asking the question, "Who do you think I am?"

Later that evening. the costume winners were judged by three of the guests who Harding and Kimber chose because they appeared to be impartial. It was agreed by everyone that the "Deeper and Deeper" team would be exempt from competing for the "Best Costume" prize.

With a big drum roll and much applause, the winners of the "Best Group Costume" were announced by opening a gold envelope that had a star shaped seal and red ribbon holding it shut: the winners of the "Best Group Costumes" were four people from the Yacht Club who came as characters from *The Wizard of Oz*, with one woman in a blue checkered dress and a white under blouse carrying a stuffed toy dog for "Toto". She finished off the costume with shoes covered with red glitter… a fun if rather *zaftig* Dorothy.

She came with three companions, one covered in aluminum foil who sported a silver funnel for a hat as the Tin Man, another as the Scarecrow with "straw" made out of paper from a paper shredder coming out of his sleeves, pants legs, and even his fly! The third was the Cowardly Lion, whose hairy costume was made from a brown Flokati rug with a rather clever homemade headpiece. The owner said he had great fun putting the costume together as he had cut up a rug that he had always hated. The costume was a triumph, except for the Lion's tail which consisted of more of the rug over a piece of flexible plumber's wire that had the unfortunate tendency of having a mind of its own and kept hitting other guests when the man turned around.

Each was awarded a dinner for two at the *Café de Paris*.

The individual award winner went to a woman dressed as Bette Davis in *Whatever Happened to Baby Jane?* She nailed the look by adding inches of makeup on her face and somehow made her hair look like the wig Davis had worn in the movie. She even carried a trowel and a small canvas bag that said, "Makeup" on it. The makeup was actually whipping cream and from time to time, she added to her makeup and occasionally took a taste of it… Disgusting and very funny. As the solo winner she won a wild round of applause and dinner for two at the *Café de Paris*.

Then Colette pointed out a small, very pretty eleven-year-old girl. Her name was Sandy and she had dressed up as *The Little Mermaid*. She told everyone that she had made the costume herself by gluing on hundreds of large blue-green sequins all over her "tail", making it full of shimmering scales. Then, with some help from her mother, she made the end of the fishtail out of some plastic that had been a shipping container for some tools her father had recently ordered. This effectively hid her tiny feet.

Her mother had helped her with her hair which had little fake starfishes entwined in her locks, and to finish off the costume she had two large seashells attached to her flesh-colored top to form a "sea bra," as she called it. Sandy also carried a large shell-like device that shot out bubbles from time to time. Sandy's mother had found it for her after Sandy had begged for bubbles, as her outfit would be "really great" if she could be surrounded by them. She was just unbelievably cute and, interestingly, Colette's Ice Queen seemed to thaw when she was interacting with little Sandy.

In the end it was decided to give Sandy a special prize for the "Most Adorable Costume." The prize was tea for four at the *Café de Paris* so she could take three of her friends out for a tea party. When the prize was awarded, Colette was seen to shed a tear, which inadvertently caused some of her ice-like makeup to dissolve and expose her real-life face as it bled through her icy visage.

Later at one point, Frans whispered into Harding's ear, "Yesterday we secretly met with the band and gave them some sheet music we were able to get at a local music store. We rehearsed with them for a number we want to perform for everyone's amusement, but we'll need some room for Natasha to dance in."

With that, Harding, sporting a huge grin, announced, "Can I have everyone's attention? Would you all please clear a space here on the dance floor? We have something very special for you."

When the space was cleared, Frans, who had slicked his hair back a la Fred Astaire, announced "I'd like to sing 'The Way You Look Tonight' by Jerome Kern with lyrics by Dorothy Fields to the most talented and beautiful lady on board, Natasha Dinara." He gestured to Natasha as she swept onto the floor to great applause.

As the band struck up, to everyone's surprise Frans had a rather pleasant voice, not great but then Fred Astaire's hadn't been that great either, and the lyrics did seem to suit their relationship. After about five bars with Frans singing and at the same time looking adoringly at Natasha, she began to dance. There she was in her white flowing gown trimmed with feathers and with her blonde hair looking the very image of Ginger Rogers. But more than that, there was a special joy to her face as if dancing was everything to her.

Was she dancing for the party crowd or just for Frans or maybe, in truth, for herself. There was such a sense of pleasure to her performance and a chemistry between singer and dancer that their enjoyment extended to the audience. It was a rare treat indeed for them to see a dance performed by a world-famous dancer so close that they could see how incredibly beautiful she was. It was also clear to everyone that the man singing to her was deeply in love with her. At the end of their number, they were rewarded with a huge volley of applause, bravos, and even a few whistles. It had been a magical moment that folks would talk about for days. It was clear that everyone was having a fantastic time.

Later in the evening, someone handed Tommy an opened bottle of champagne, which he absent-mindedly set aside. After the party was over, he spotted the bottle and, rather than let it go to waste, took it to the crew's lounge and put it in the fridge with a silver spoon in it, as his mother had once told him that by putting a spoon in the bottle, the champagne would "hold." He then promptly forgot about the bottle.

The party continued to be a huge success and went on to 2:00 AM. After the last guest left, the Klieg lights were turned off, the food and drink put away, and the party glasses and plates were moved to the galley. Lew had seen Ali as the last guest left, but later was unable to find her. No matter how much everyone looked for her, she didn't turn up.

It wasn't until after 3:30 AM when Suzanne, while taking some of the cloth cocktail napkins into the laundry room, let out a blood-curdling scream. Everyone, who had been having a final drink in the forward salon, came rushing to see what the commotion was about only to find Suzanne standing over Ali's body. which was lying on the floor in a contorted position, her head resting at an odd angle and one of her shoes off. Her eyes were wide open with a look of surprise on them and there was blood everywhere!

This was met with stunned silence, as it was clear that Ali was dead, VERY dead.

Had she fallen? What was she doing in the laundry room in the first place? And what the hell had happened? Harding quickly pulled out his phone and tried to call the police. Frantically, he said, "Does anyone know if 911 works here in Monte Carlo?"

"Never mind, Monsieur, I'll take care of this" said the first mate Olivier. He took out his cellphone and called the police. He also took a series of photos of the scene "Just in case."

Within ten minutes or so they heard police sirens approach and, with much screeching of brakes, the police arrived and were ushered onto the yacht and into the laundry room. There were two very officious men who immediately took charge of the scene. They were in there a long time and, after taking numerous photos themselves, it was determined that it had been one of those unfortunate accidents and Ali's body was finally removed on a stretcher, placed in a waiting ambulance, and taken to a nearby funeral while everyone remained in the lounge in stunned silence. Lew, in particular seemed unable to speak. Finally, he said in a daze, "Why was she in the laundry room? Did she slip? Trip? God, why did this have to happen?" It all seemed surreal, what with him still looking like Oliver Hardy, his fake moustache at an odd angle on his perspiring face.

The police appeared to believe that she had accidentally fallen, hit the front of her head, knocked herself unconscious and bled to death. Nevertheless, they took down everyone's names and remained on the boat. It was noted that Ali had been seen after all the guests left, so if there had been any foul play, it would have been the work of one of the guests still on board the "Deeper and Deeper."

After the ambulance left with Ali's body and the police departed, there was a bizarre silence amongst the yacht's occupants. Slowly people drifted off to their cabins and the yacht took on a strange, eerie silence and a feeling as if life had been drained from the very life of the boat. The festive party decorations hung in their respective places, mocking the fact that life had dramatically changed. A large photo of Bette Davis from All About Eve looked down on the after-party remains with a look that said, "Just you wait and see what's in store for you!"

For some of the boat's occupants this time would end

up being one of those brief dramatic moments to relate to others in years to come but for a few, it was an event that would impact their lives forever.

Harding, of course, was deeply concerned and after trying to make sense of what had just transpired and, having failed completely, he headed off to his cabin. Once there, he slowly started to get ready for bed in the hopes that he might be able to sleep, a doubtful possibility. Deep in thought, he took his gun from his waistband, stared at it a bit and finally placed it in the safe and put the whip on a nearby chair. He then took off his boots, torn shirt, and khaki pants. Stripped down to his shorts, he lowered the lights.

Suddenly there was a soft knock on his door. He went over and opened it and there stood Kimber in one of the bathrobes that came with each cabin. Without saying a word, she stepped forward and was soon embraced in his arms. They stayed that way, just holding each other for a long, long time, she to gather strength from this man whom she was quickly becoming attached to and he to comfort and yes, hopefully gain strength from this amazing woman. They suddenly needed each other, and the need was desperate and deep.

Without saying a word, he slowly and gently lifted her up and placed her on the bed as her robe fell away, revealing her beautiful breasts. He gently kissed her and then started to work his mouth and hands all over her body. As he did this, it was as if he was awakening a need in Kimber that she hadn't realized was there, a need that had not been addressed in the past few years. Here was a man, someone special, who might just be the one element in life she was missing.

The only sounds now were low moans that occasionally escaped her lips. Both were suddenly aware that each wanted to be a comfort to the other person. There was a thrill knowing that they were both alive and connected in their need to put death out of sight. It was both comforting and at the same time extraordinarily exhilarating, almost a celebration of life!

And so, this death in a strange way brought a new form of life to the two. Both had grown to appreciate the other and now to rely on the other for comfort and companionship. It was the beginning of a new phase in their relationship, one that gave more depth and meaning to each other.

Later, as they laid in each other's arms, Kimber said, "You seem so *bien dans sa, peau…* grounded. How did you get that way?"

Harding smiled and looked thoughtful and finally said, "I was lucky. I had a mother who was incredibly wise. She had several favorite sayings: One was: 'There is no freedom without responsibility.' and believe me, I learned to be very responsible at an early very age as I wanted my freedom!"

Smiling, he went on to say, "She also used to say, 'If a job is worth doing, it's worth doing well.' The only problem with that is one is sometimes faced with a job that appears to be worthwhile doing, but in the long run it's not worth the effort. Ah, the nuances of life! She also used to say, 'If there is no solution, there's no problem.' That said, we possess a problem here and we must find a solution… who caused Ali's death? Who murdered her… and believe me, I firmly believe she was killed. There are just too many unexplained elements to her death regardless of what the police think. We have to find out who the perpetrator is. We're all in great danger as there could possibly more murders."

This was met by silence.

"On another level, I feel like taking on this yacht has probably been a big mistake. The longer we're on this boat, the less it appeals to me with the exception of my being enamored of you as you've become more integrated into my life. I want to share my life with you."

Kimber smiled at these thoughts, as each brought her closer to understanding this interesting and complicated man. She certainly was on the same page when it came to the feelings that they had for one another. She, too, was finding herself being drawn closer and closer into this special union.

While they talked, she stroked his head and suddenly felt an indentation. Out of curiosity asked, "What caused that?"

There was a long pause and finally, Harding said, "Oh, I had a problem… a problem with balance and how it affected my walking."

Kimber looked at him with concern.

"So, I got worried and asked my doctor about it, and he in turn set up an appointment with The Cleveland Clinic."

Again, there was a long pause and Harding finally said in kind of a sheepish way, "Years ago I kind of became a donor there and so I get special treatment. It was determined that I had hydrocephalus. In layman's terms, it's a case where an excessive amount of fluid builds up within one's brain cavities, causing one's ventricles to widen, which puts harmful pressure on the tissues of one's brain… hence the balance problem. There is no cure, but there is a treatment. The treatment was to have brain surgery, compliments of Dr. Ron Ward,

"He, in case you haven't heard, is one of the top brain surgeons in the nation. It was considerably disconcerting for me to have someone drill into my brain… really scary but unfortunately necessary. But, as you can see, I'm just fine. Clearly, he solved my problem and I have been extremely grateful ever since. That's one of the reasons Ron and his wife Jenny are on board. It's kind of a payback… a thank you and a way in which I can find out more about his work, as I think I'd like to contribute MORE to the Clinic if it turns out to be a good idea. Since the operation, he and

I have become sort of friends and I've made several donations to his hospital. A pretty good tradeoff, I'd say. I got my balance back and they got some much-needed money to balance the hospital's budget."

Kimber reached over, and gently and lovingly caressed his head, and gave him a tender kiss on the indented part. "I might regret saying this to you, Harding, but I find myself loving you… more than yesterday and I believe less than tomorrow."

Harding smiled, "Yes, I feel the same." He took the watch he had bought at the Paris flea market that was on the nightstand, looked at the time and said, "I can't believe the time. Where did it go?"

Kimber grinned as he put the watch back on the nightstand and with that, the long day finally caught up with the two of them and they drifted off to sleep in each other's arms. They did this knowing that something special and extraordinary had just transpired between them and that their relationship had moved towards a new and exciting plane.

Chapter Six
Unanswered Questions

The next few days were a blank. It was as if the world had been put on hold. Nothing seemed to happen, but of course, that wasn't true, it just appeared that way. The occupants on "Deeper and Deeper" seemed to exist in a daze or a thick fog. Oh, the world went on, the remains of the party were dealt with, and the photos of the guests which had been taken by a hired company went out with a printed message thanking the recipients for helping to make the party such a success. The boat was cleaned up and returned to what should have been normal, but there was no longer any normalcy to life on "Deeper and Deeper." There was just a suspension of time until the shock of the aftermath of the party and Ali's death wore off.

Harding, in particular, waited for some response from the police, as he was convinced that Ali's passing was no accident. But when he probed, he found that the police reported her death as "A mishap", that "Mrs. Ali Adelman had fallen, hit her head, and bled to death." To Harding that made no sense.

Having an instinct to spot and solve problems, he remembered his childhood friend Harvey Willis, who was now—as an adult—known as Inspector Willis who had a detective agency named "The 3 in 1 Investigating Agency". Harding promptly contacted Willis and, within a matter of hours, Willis and his assistants Ross and Monty were hired and on the next plane headed for Monte Carlo.

Both Harding and Kimber had a feeling that the fog which had engulfed the yacht was lifting a bit and that a sense of control might be returning to "Deeper and Deeper". It was a feeling of relief that felt good, if somewhat tentative.

The next morning, Inspector Willis and his two assistants landed at the airport and were picked up by Mac and driven to the yacht. Harding was waiting on the stern area of the deck in anticipation of their arrival, and on meeting Willis, Ross, and Monty, Harding was effusive in his joy of seeing his childhood friend. "It's so good to see you, Willis. I can't thank you enough for coming here on such short notice. I trust these two gentlemen here are your assistants."

"Yup," said Willis. "Meet Monty and Ross Anderson, two finer men you'll never meet. Bet you'll have fun telling these two identical twins apart."

The four men proceeded to shake hands, and with that, Harding said. "Good to meet you two. Thanks all of you for coming. My partner Kimber, whom you'll soon meet, and I very much appreciate it."

Willis replied, "It's a pleasure, Harding. After all, we were such good friends when we were teens before we went our separate ways."

Harding, gesturing towards Willis, said, "I wonder if you two ever heard about the shenanigans this man pulled in his youth. He was a real cutup as a teen." Turning towards Willis he said, "Remember the canoe trip we took in Canada while we were in the Boy Scouts? We were what, maybe seventeen? We paddled across an endless number of lakes which provided really glorious vistas, but it was the portages—that is, carrying everything from lake to lake—that was the killer. We took turns. One would carry the canoe and the other our backpacks which contained our tent, food, and personal items. I remember two things in particular about that trip. First, I remember that Willis here managed to always carry the light stuff on the long portages. First he carried the canoe, which was the lighter of the two items, but as we used up our provisions the backpacks became the lighter items, and suddenly he was carrying them! I never could figure out how you managed that! And second was the incredible forest of white birch trees we passed through one day. It was unbelievably beautiful… pure magic! To this day, when I see a birch tree, I think of our wonderful time together and that magical forest!" With that. Harding gave Willis a pat on his shoulder.

"Enough of that," Willis said. "… to business. You need to know that our company, the '3 in 1 Investigating Agency' consists of just me and my two assistants here. We formed the company four years ago with the express purpose of investigating and solving murders. That said, I think it best if we get settled in and then get to work on the case here."

Looking at Harding, Willis said, "You explained the situation here to me over the phone. Would it be possible to see the scene of Ali's death and then to meet with Lew?"

As the men were talking, Tommy gave Mac a hand with the luggage. It had been decided that Ross and Monty would take the last stateroom and that Willis would use Harding's office as a combination office and cabin, as there was a Murphy bed built into the side wall and a full head. Harding would use the desk in his own cabin for his personal office work.

Harding helped Willis, Ross, and Monty get settled in.

Two extra chairs were added to the dining room table for Ross and Monty, and Willis was given Ali's now-vacant chair. Soon Kimber joined the men, was introduced, and they all went down to the laundry room.

When they got there, Harding produced a key that was on a hook hidden out of sight nearby and unlocked the door. He then said, "This lock is new. I asked Philip to arrange to have it put on after Ali died to secure the area." He then opened a folder he was carrying and said, "Here are some photos of Ali's body that Olivier took before it was removed… and a good thing too, because the police are taking the stand that it was all an accident, that Ali had fallen, hit her head, and bled to death. It was doubtful that the police would willingly release copies of what I'm now calling 'the crime scene.'"

As the men looked around the room, they could see the traces of Ali's dried blood that were still everywhere.

Willis soon asked, "Do you know what happened to her body?"

Harding replied, "Since the police determined that her death had been an accident, her body was released to the Tari Funeral Home, which is nearby and one that the police recommended."

"Before I talk to Lew, can you walk us through the events leading up to the discovery of her body?"

"Certainly," said Harding. As they walked around the

boat, Harding said, "For the party, we moved out most of the furniture here on the aft deck so the guests could dance to a small band I hired. There were about 40 guests plus the folks who were living and working on the yacht. We also hired some additional help, including two bartenders, a photographer, several waitresses and waiters, plus a local TV personality whose job was to interview arriving guests, security and such, probably 80-odd folks in all."

Harding had arranged for many of the photos of the party to be printed. As he showed them to Willis and company, he continued, "As you can see from these photos, it was a costume party where everyone was to come as a famous person from the movies. The idea was that everyone would make his or her own costume. No rented costumes. All the guests arrived over there starting around 9:00 PM." as he pointed to the stern area of the yacht. As he showed Willis, Ross, and Monty the photos, he pointed out the various people from the boat and described their costumes.

In several of the photos Ali appeared first smiling and dancing, and then later she looked very serious. Kimber found it quite curious. She wondered if Ali had any inkling as to what was in store for her. At one point it looked like she had removed her hat as her Laurel character and Willis asked, "What happened to her hat? It certainly wasn't in the laundry room. It's important that we find out what happened to it."

The men soon began to grasp the situation and the people who participated in the party. Harding explained, "As I said, the party started at 9:00 that evening and broke up at 2:00 AM... The last of the guests left and Ali was still alive at that point in time. It was then, after the party had wound down and everyone had a final drink or were just chatting about the night's events, that Suzanne found Ali's body in the laundry room a bit after 3:00 AM, I'd say... probably more like 3:20 or so."

Willis then asked Monty, "Please set up a meeting for me to go to the funeral home to view the body. Meanwhile, let's meet her husband and hear what he has to say."

Harding brought Willis, Ross, and Monty down to Lew's cabin. They knocked on the cabin door and a very sober Lew answered and ushered them in. At first it seemed like a bad idea as the cabin, while spacious for two people, was rather crowded for the five of them. However, everyone found a place to sit with the two brothers ending up sitting on the edge of the foot of the bed. Harding insisted on remaining standing.

After being introduced, Willis said to Lew, "Tell us in your own words what happened the night Ali died."

Lew was at first very quiet, seeming lost in thought, and then proceeded to talk as in a dream. "It had been a wonderful night," he said. "You wouldn't believe the excitement, the fun that everyone was having. Ali and I got caught up in the fun of the party. While our 'Hollywood' costumes as Laurel and Hardy weren't as creative as some of the others, we nevertheless had a great time as those two characters. I had made a little moustache for myself out of a piece of black tape I got from Olivier, the first mate, so that I'd look like Oliver Hardy. Ali had a bit of a problem, because portraying Stan Laurel she had to hide her hair, but she somehow got black hats for both of us, and she did an excellent job of hiding her hair and the rest was easy... bowties and men's jackets for each of us did the trick."

As he said this, he gestured towards a black hat that was casually hooked on the edge of the dressing table mirror. "Anyway, we looked pretty darn good, but we weren't nearly as creative as some of the others. You should have seen Harry's costume of Jack Nicholson in *One Flew Over the Cuckoo's Nest*. Anyway, we were having a great time when suddenly Ali got sort of sullen, I don't know why. She just got edgy and kind of, I don't know… strange. And then she disappeared. My guess is she came here to our cabin as I found her hat here later on. After that, I don't know what happened. It wasn't until much later that we found her... Her body in the laundry room..."

His voice trailed off. After a few deep breaths, he said, "I don't know why she went to the laundry room. I didn't even know it existed. How could she have fallen and knocked herself out and ended up bleeding to death?" The poor man seemed crestfallen and at a complete loss.

Willis walked over to pick up the hat and looked it over carefully. As he inspected the hatband, he saw a piece of paper sticking out and very carefully pulled it out, unfolded it and read the following message typed in capital letters:

MEET ME IN THE LAUNDRY ROOM OR I'LL TELL EVERYONE EVERYTHING!

He quickly showed it to Monty and Ross, and then said to Lew, "Do you mind if I search your cabin? I suspect that your wife's death was no accident. "

Lew hesitated as if unable to make up his mind, and then solemnly nodded his head "Okay," as it clearly would look like he had something to hide if he refused. He, however, did not look happy. Willis, Ross, and Monty proceeded to go over the cabin with a fine-toothed comb but found nothing of importance.

Willis next asked Harding for a list of everyone who was living on the yacht as well as a list of the guests who attended the party. The latter proved unnecessary, as it had been determined that Ali had been seen after the last guest had left. Consequently, it was clear that Ali had fallen and bled to death sometime after 2:00 AM. Next, Willis took the list of the persons living on the boat and set up a schedule to interview everyone, but not before visiting the funeral parlor to view Ali's body.

The funeral home or *salon funéraire* was a short drive away, and Willis asked Lew to accompany him so there wouldn't be a problem with viewing the body. Arrangements had yet to be made for Ali's burial or cremation, so her body should still be intact and basically undisturbed. Mac drove them to the funeral home and told them to take their time, as he would be nearby. He then gave Willis his business card and suggested that Willis call him when they needed a ride back to the yacht.

Willis and Lew got out of the car and walked up the steps to the funeral home. The reception room was a sober environment with grey walls, heavy grey drapes to match, and rather formal heavily upholstered chairs in small groups with a reception desk being the major point of focus. Behind the desk was a woman in a severe dark grey suit and an expression to match. Having overheard the men speaking in English, she addressed them in a rather formal English with a slight French accent, asking, "May I be of some help, gentlemen?"

Willis replied, gesturing towards Lew. "This is Mr. Lew Adelman and I'm Inspector Willis. We have come to see the remains of Ali Adelman, this gentleman's wife."

The receptionist said, "I hope you'll understand but I need some sort of identification."

To which Willis nodded, indicating that he understood, and Lew and Willis produced their passports.

"You realize, of course, that we have to be cautious about such things."

After looking at the passports, the woman nodded her head, returned them, and pushed a buzzer on the desk, which soon produced a gentleman in a dark blue pinstriped suit whom she introduced as Monsieur Colom. She proceeded to tell him in French to show the two gentlemen the remains of Ali Adelman. The men were then led through a door, down a flight of stairs into a large, gray room that was very cold and devoid of any furnishings. The room had a light, peculiar odor and the lighting was such as it didn't produce any shadows. Willis couldn't help thinking that it smelled faintly like an animal rotting, a disturbing thought at best. Having been in similar places like this, he knew this was common.

On one wall was a series of large file cabinets, each was about three feet wide by 30 inches high stacked two high with maybe ten across. There were labels with names attached to some of the cabinets. Monsieur Colom then approached one cabinet which had Ali's name on it. "Would you like to see the remains?" which seemed a rather odd request, since they obviously were there to do just that. When both men nodded "yes", Monsieur Colom pulled the cabinet open to reveal a body covered entirely with a white sheet except for two feet that were exposed, one with an identification tag wired to one of the toes with the name

"Ali Adelman" written on it in block letters in black ink. The gentleman then pulled the sheet back to reveal Ali's face, which was lacking in color.

Her hair had been combed back away from her face, which revealed the gash on the front of her head which had caused her to bleed to death. She lay there with her eyes wide open but clouded over. There remained some dried blood on the side of her head.

Monsieur Colom then quietly went over to a corner and left the two men alone. Willis then reached over and pulled the fabric further down as Lew gasped. Ali's breasts were pierced with two small gold rods and her breasts were severely bruised.

Lew exclaimed, "I... I Don't understand. What happened to her breasts and what are those rod-like things sticking in her nipples?"

Willis replied, "Those are nipple piercings, but surely you have seen them before. Do you have any idea how she got bruised that way?"

There was a long pause before Lew responded and, floundering, said, "Actually, I've never seen Ali's breasts. We had a platonic relationship. I… I never saw her nude. I… I just assumed she was modest and not interested in sex. We were kinda like brother and sister… a partnership… a very puritanical relationship." Lew paused and then said, "Oh, she could be difficult and bossy, but I loved her. We were a good team." He paused. "I'm so confused. How would she have gotten those bruises?"

Willis asked, "Did Ali have any close friends other than you?"

"No, not really. A few lady friends back home but as for here on the boat, just Harding's guests and crew and, as you know, we just met them a few days ago. I… I'm so confused. I just don't understand."

"Well, those bruises look to have been made recently. If we can find out who injured her breasts that way, we might well find out who killed her. I'm pretty sure that her death was no accident."

With this last comment by Willis, Lew turned away and refused to look at Ali anymore. Willis double-checked and the bruises were certainly recent. He then proceeded to examine the rest of Ali's body, but found nothing out of the ordinary except a small tattoo of two women kissing that was located on her upper inner right thigh in a manner to be kept out of sight. He quickly took a small sample of her hair, as he had the foresight to bring a small pair of scissors with him and an envelope to hold the hair sample. He also took several photos with his iPhone. He then pulled the sheet back over Ali's body and called Monsieur Colom to tell him that they were through. Ali's body was then rolled back into the wall and the three men left.

Once they were back in the reception area, Willis

thanked Monsieur Colom and they both shook his hand and left the building. As the two men walked down the outside steps, they were greeted by the warmth of the sunny day and it almost said, "Welcome back to life!" Willis then took out his phone and, with the business card Mac had given him, called Mac and said that they were ready to be picked up. Within a matter of moments, Mac pulled the car up and they were soon on their way back to the yacht.

Lew was extremely quiet on the ride back to the yacht. Occasionally, he would start to say something, would pause, then change his mind. He would then quietly shake his head in disbelief. He finally said, "It's probably nothing but for some reason or other, Ali seemed annoyed at Suzanne the other day."

"In what way?" asked Willis.

"Oh, I don't know ... My sense is that Ali was angry with her, but then Ali was often annoyed at people."

Later that afternoon, Willis found Lew alone on the stern of the yacht and casually asked, "Mind if I join you?"

Lew shrugged, and while he didn't seem particularly defensive, he certainly wasn't friendly towards Willis. "How are you holding up?" asked Willis.

"What do you think, Inspector?" I'm totally wiped out if you want the truth. I feel like I've been hit with, I don't know... Some invisible enemy seems to have entered my life and I don't know how to defend myself." As he said this, he took out a handkerchief from his pants pocket and wiped his sweating brow.

Willis nodded and quietly sat there with him. After a while, Willis said, "I'm so sorry for your loss. It must be very difficult for you." When Lew didn't respond, Willis gently asked, "How did you and Ali meet?"

At first Willis wondered if Lew had heard his question, as Lew didn't seem to respond, but then suddenly, he said in sort of a dream-like voice, "We met in school. It was 22 years ago, and we were both going to Hofstra University, studying theatre. Ali was 20 at the time and I was 31. Prior to school, I had been a marine and spent time in some really rough situations. I know, looking at my big belly you'd never suspect that I had been a marine and capable of jumping out of planes and fighting, but I was very young and the marines had whipped me into shape. A good thing too, as I had some very rough experiences during the liberation of Kuwait. Experiences which I never talk about. Suffice it to say I saw and did some pretty horrific things as a young man." There was a long pause when a strange look came across Lew's face.

After a while, Lew seemed to refocus on the moment and proceeded to say "Anyway, fast forward, Ali and I both came from lower middle-class families and Hofstra was a community university for us. Because we had so many interests in common, Ali and I gravitated towards each other, started dating, and eventually married... No children. Because it was next to impossible to make any money in theatre, upon graduation we decided to try our luck in television. Ali got a job working on a soap… a soap opera, and I got a job as a glorified runner on a talk show… you know, delivering schedules, scripts, and so forth. It was hard work with very little pay, but we made contacts and along the way we had a good time. Both of us were very ambitious, not afraid of work, and, yeah, smart. We were good partners. Slowly we moved our way up to some assistant producer type jobs. After a while, we were eventually able to produce some industrials and even a big telethon on our own."

"Then one day we came up with an idea for a game show that was really terrific. We pitched it to the networks and had the idea stolen right out from under us. We were livid, especially Ali. One never crossed Ali if one valued one's life. And so, we sharpened our defenses, came up with other production ideas, and finally got one of them produced: a game show called "What Do You Know?" with Harry King as the host. While it's not an intellectual triumph, it somehow resonates with the public. We've been on the air for six years now with no end in sight."

"To date, we've sold the show to the English, French, and Germans and have a deal in the works to sell it to the Japanese. We're doing... We were doing really well. We got the typical large mansion in Beverly Hills and had a top decorator do the décor. We even hired an English butler with dreams of having a lot of big Hollywood parties but, I don't know, somehow, they never materialized. Ali and I don't have... Didn't have many friends. Anyway, we were really enjoying the work and our success. And now... I just don't understand. I thought Ali's death was just a freak accident, life's way of saying 'Your good fortune is over.'"

Willis looked deep into Lew's eyes and saw a man totally lost, as if all life had been drained out of him.

Willis felt that while Lew and Ali's careers had been wildly successful, he doubted that their marriage could have been all that fulfilling. He was at a loss as to what to say to Lew and ultimately just gave him a comforting squeeze on his shoulder and then quietly left him.

With no particular person in mind, Willis went into the lounge and found himself in Natasha's company. She was drinking a large glass of water, was wearing a leotard in a cheery yellow and white pattern, and looked like she had just finished a workout as she clearly had worked up quite a sweat.

Willis looked at her admiringly. He always responded to people who had a sense of discipline, which clearly was the case with Natasha. There was no way that she could have reached the degree of success that she enjoyed without the dedication and determination that her profession demanded. After a brief chat, Willis and she agreed to meet in a half hour or so after she had a shower. As she headed down to her cabin, Willis went to his temporary office.

There he found Monty, who had brought his computer up and was poring over it.

"I moved up here for a while so I could do some research, as Ross is using our cabin to talk to Harry," Monty muttered. "From what I gather, Jenny was with Kimber the latter part of the evening as Jenny's a Francophile, speaks French, and loves talking about international politics. While talking to her, I found out that she and her husband have been married for 32 years. It turns out she worked to help put Harry through medical school and then had three kids."

"Not satisfied with that, with the kids away at school and Harry making good money, she went back to school. First, to study French, and then with the idea of doing grad work to become a lawyer. Interesting enough, she didn't go that route, as a friend, upon hearing that she was thinking of becoming a lawyer, had a dinner party for her and invited several female lawyers."

"Jenny recalled that one of the ladies in particular was adamant about how difficult it was for a woman to go that route. She made it clear that Jenny would have to dress a certain way, use subtle makeup, and that she would have to be a hell of a lot smarter than her fellow male lawyers to succeed. Upon hearing this, Jenny decided that she would be damned if she would adjust her image to please a bunch of male lawyers. It turned out she was one very smart, ambitious lady and, instead, studied to be a therapist and apparently became a remarkably fine one. Is she capable of killing someone? Possibly, but I can't find a reason that would connect her to the victim."

"Meanwhile, I've found some interesting information about Natasha. It seems that while she sports a Russian-sounding background, she is a hundred percent American. As a young girl, she was close to her maternal grandmother who came from Russia and taught Natasha to speak Russian, but our little dancer's real name is Karen Obolensky. At 13 years old she went to study ballet at the Royal Ballet School in London and took on the first name of Natasha along with a slight Russian accent. Apparently, it was an excellent move on her part, as there is still to this day a certain cachet of having Russian roots as a ballet dancer. What else she had edited about her life remains to be seen."

"As for Colette... at first, I thought she might have been antagonistic towards Ali, as Ali had verbally attacked her about her appearance. Apparently, Ali was very blunt and had upset Colette a great deal. I checked Colette out and she left the party along with the guests, according to Tommy and Olivier, so it is doubtful that she could have returned and attacked Ali without others having seen her return to the yacht."

Willis smiled as he loved to see his partners in action and being such a help. In many ways, Ross and Monty were like the sons he never had, and he was inordinately proud of them. He then got up, secured a cup of coffee and went up on deck and waited for Natasha to reappear, which she soon did. She was in an all-white outfit that consisted of shorts, a man's shirt that was tied above her waist which exposed a flat, firm stomach, no shoes, and she had on a baseball cap that made her look like she was in her late 20's—roughly half her real age.

"So how is your inspection going, Inspector?" she asked in kind of a teasing way.

Realizing instantly that her question came off as flip and insensitive, she quickly corrected herself by saying, "That came out all wrong. I'm sincerely interested in knowing what's going on. Did Ali have an accident or was she murdered? There are all sorts of rumors flying around here."

"I assure you I didn't misunderstand you. My partners Monty and Ross and I are here to find out if there was any foul play, as Harding seems to feel there was. Tell me, how did you happen to be here on this yacht?"

"Hmmm, a good question. Actually, I'm not so sure why we're here. I met Harding at a dinner party and we got to talking. And one thing led to another." With that, Willis tilted his head as though she had revealed something interesting and useful.

"No, not that way. What I meant was, Harding and I sort of clicked. We liked each other right off the bat." This latter comment sounded odd, it being a bit of a slang term which didn't quite fit with her slight Russian accent. "We have some things in common in that we both came from very little but have had some wonderful successes. His financially and me in the world of dance."

"Tell me about your world, Natasha," Willis asked, looking her directly in the eye. "How did you get to be so successful, so famous?"

Natasha's face broke out in a huge smile. "Well, without sounding full of myself, I worked very hard, really hard. But you know, there are many others in my profession who are as dedicated as I've been but," she shrugged, "One has to have a God-given talent as well as determination and, of course, good timing always helps. I was lucky to have the talent AND the opportunity to develop that talent. As long as I can remember, I wanted to dance. At age four, I was already taking dance lessons, as my mother was very ambitious for me. The dance school I was enrolled in was, how shall I put it… the school was unbelievably unprofessional. They actually put me en pointe at the age of seven, which usually results in ruining a child's feet. A short time later, my mother found a better school for me. Luckily, I hadn't suffered any real damage to my feet."

"When I was twelve my parents pushed to get me into the Royal Ballet School in London. They took me over to England and, after auditioning with the school, I was accepted. Imagine, I left home at the age of twelve and began living at the boarding school called White Lodge, where Queen Victoria used to go as a child. I loved it there, what with its beautiful gardens and challenging schooling. This is where I wanted to be… Where I was meant to be and where I started my real training. Can you believe me leaving home at that early age? The simple fact was I had to dance. I never had a choice. In my mind dancing was everything. Still is, but now, as I'm getting too old to dance, I'm kind of at a loss as to what to do. What will become of me?"

"Anyway, after my training was completed, I was lucky enough to get into the Royal Danish Ballet, a remarkable company for such a small country. The company was and continues to be well known and highly respected. It also was small enough for me to shine in it, you know, get roles that not only made me look good but also helped me develop into a respected star in my field. I stayed there a number of years and established my reputation and then, when I was ready and fully established, I broke away and have been, how would you put it, freelancing ever since. I've stayed with several companies for a season or more but I've been on my own for years or so it seems. I tend to be offered guest appearances with various ballet companies. It's not as glamorous as it sounds, as it means constantly moving from company to company, adjusting to each new situation."

"I don't know," said Willis. "I saw you perform with the Joffrey Ballet Company say, maybe four or five years ago and you were remarkable. I have to say it's an honor to have met you."

"Thank you for that. In truth, I'm constantly having to watch my back, as there are always jealous people waiting in the wings and wanting my roles. Along the way I met Alexander Woulf, who was a great impresario. While I can't say that it was a great romantic alliance, we nevertheless got married as we suited each other. He liked to mould talent and careers, and I needed someone to take charge of mine. I was… am a great dancer, but that's all. I have no skills at promoting myself, handling money, and so forth. Alexander was a Godsend. He made me famous and secure. Unfortunately, he was considerably older than me and one evening six years ago he had a massive heart attack and died."

"I was left… not destitute but with little ability to take care of myself on many levels, including financially. I made some bad financial choices and with my career almost over, I'm in my early 40's, I try to be careful and plan accordingly. It's strange, after all that success, I feel like I'm in a holding pattern with no place to go but down. As for Ali, I didn't care for her in the slightest. She actually made a pass at me which not only surprised me, it frightened me. In a rather bizarre way, I think that maybe Ali was lucky. She was successful, seemed to have had a good marriage—well, maybe, maybe not, at least a good partnership and then made a clean exit. I wonder..." And it appeared that Natasha had little more to say on the subject.

Willis smiled. "I think your story is remarkable and I have great respect for you, your talent and fortitude. Thank you so much for sharing your thoughts and time. I've very much enjoyed talking to you. Now if you'll please excuse me, I have some work I need to address."

Willis next found Ross and explained that he wanted a collection of fingerprints from everyone on the yacht without their being aware of it. One suggestion he made was to collect drink glasses from the next time everyone was having a cocktail party. That would take care of the guests. Getting sample fingerprints from the crew would be a bit more challenging, but Willis knew how clever Monty could be in situations such as this.

It took Monty a while, but by the end of the day, he had a box that was carefully packed with items that were labeled and had sample fingerprints of everyone on the "Deeper and Deeper". Willis then had it shipped to a lab where a record of everyone's prints would be filed. Willis said that this was just a precautionary move and that he felt in his guts that these sample prints might come in handy, and he wanted to be prepared.

Later, Willis went to his office. When he got there, he sat down at the desk, took out his computer, and made the following list of potential killers, in no particular order:

Harding West
Kimber Lepelletier
Lew Adelman
Natasha Dinara
Frans Klamer
Ron Ward
Jenny Ward

The crew:

Philip Molina – the captain
Olivier Tari – the first mate
Tommy Klez – the second mate
Claude Seyrat – head steward
Suzanne Seyrat – Steward and Claude's wife
Tony Blom—the ship's engineer
Mac Mc Kinley -the chauffeur
Colette Napier – the party planner

Since it was established that Ali was seen saying goodbye to the last guest as they were leaving the yacht, the list of suspects was narrowed down to just the above list, but Colette and Mac were removed, as she had left with the rest of the guests when the party was over and Mac had delivered three guests to their home and had retired for the night.

Going down his list of people to interview, he checked off Natasha, as he had already talked to her extensively. Next, he assigned Monty to interview Frans. He then intended to have his team talk to Kimber, Jenny, and Harry Ward. He also needed to have them talk to the yacht's staff.

Shortly after, Monty approached Frans as he was headed towards the aft deck of the yacht. Frans was in a pair of bright blue swim trunks, had a towel, a book, and some sunscreen in hand and it was clear that his intention was to read and work on his tan.

Monty caught up with him and said casually, "Is it okay if we talk a bit while you're sunning?"

"Not a problem. I was planning to read a bit, but that can wait," Frans replied. "Will this do?" He gestured to two chaises.

Monty replied, "Sure, why not."

Once they got settled down, Monty said, "Where were you around 2:00 AM after the last guest left?"

Frans said, "I thought of helping the ship's crew take some of the decorations down, but was told by Harding that the crew would take care of it and that I should relax or go to bed. Consequently, Natasha and I decided to have a nightcap and sat on the aft deck, actually right here where we're sitting now. We talked for a bit, reliving that terrific party before going to bed."

"So can I assume that the two of you were together that whole period after the guests had left until Ali was found in the laundry room?"

"Yes, sad, isn't it. While I can't say I liked her very much, as I don't like pushy people who are full of themselves. However, it is sad. I wonder… She must have slipped or fallen. Someone said that the other day there was a bar of soap left on the floor of the laundry room and, consequently, the floor was on the slippery side. It's all hard to imagine."

Monty responded, "I guess that could have been the case, but odd that she would be in the laundry room in the first place." After a pause and wishing to change the subject, he said, "Tell me, Frans, how did you end up being here on this boat?"

"I actually was invited as Natasha's guest. When she got the invitation, she was a bit nervous about being alone in a strange environment with a host she hardly knew, so I suppose I was kind of an insurance policy… a way to keep her safe. Little did we know that there would be a death… A real surprise after the success of that terrific party."

"So have you known Natasha long?" Monty asked.

"Oh, I'd say around a little over a year. We met at one

of the dance studios in New York, one that's located on the West Side in the 20's, you know, where dancers rehearse. I kind of was playing the piano and Natasha was taking classes there. After a class one day, we went for a cup of coffee and, to our surprise, we hit it off. To me it was amazing, as we have such different backgrounds."

"So, you're a piano player?"

"Amongst other things. I've played the piano most of my life. I had hoped to be a concert pianist, but I had an accident while working with some power tools, and while I can still play, I hurt my right hand to the extent that I'm hampered just enough to ruin my chances of being a concert pianist."

"Can one make enough money as a pianist at dancing studios?" Monty asked.

"Well, I do other things." And he tried to leave it at that, but Monty persisted and said, "Tell me."

Sighing, he went on to say, "I really started with nothing. My father left one month before I was born. You can probably imagine how that impacted me as I was growing up. My mother… well, let's just say she wasn't very good at the maternal thing. She just didn't get it and so I learned early on to take care of myself. I kind of raised myself. Because I work out at the gym a lot, I'm in good shape."

"While in the process of working out, I learned a great deal about the human body and took some courses in giving massages, and so started doing that as well. I like it because I like taking care of people. The problem is, and I shouldn't be telling you this... but what the hell: I often would have men who I was massaging come on to me. You know, wanting to have sex with me. So, I started giving massages with both the client and myself in the nude, and one thing would lead to another and, quite truthfully, I do really well financially because of it. Of course, I do women as well, but that's a bit tricky as women tend to be nervous about allowing a male masseuse do more than just massage them. But you'd be amazed how the word gets around among the ladies and I have to tell you, not only do I enjoy my work, I feel I help people a lot... Both men and women. I have an ability to make people feel good about themselves."

"For example, and you won't believe this, last month I was working on a guy who was probably in his late 60's and as usually happens, he got an erection. Well, the guy seemed very self-conscious. He finally blurted out that he was so embarrassed that he was so small in the penis department, to which I said: 'What gives you that idea?' He said that when he was a young man, someone told him that he was ridiculously small, and he had been self-conscious and miserable about the size of his cock ever since. Well, I told him that his equipment was just fine, that he had nothing to be ashamed of, and the poor guy just broke down and sobbed. He said, 'All these years I've always felt embarrassed and thought less of myself." So, as you can see, I can help others, and consequently I feel good about myself and my work. No, I'll never be a great pianist but I'm productive, I enjoy my work. I'm proud that I help people. Thank God I'm highly sexed, but most important, I respect who I am."

That tells me a lot about this guy, thought Monty. *Off hand, I would say it's highly unlikely that both Natasha and Frans could be jointly involved in Ali's death. I'm fairly sure that there are others who saw the two of them together between the time that the guests left and Ali's death was discovered.*

"Thank you very much, Frans," Monty said as he got up to leave. "What you've told me is very helpful and extremely interesting. I must tell you that I respect you."

That took care of part of the yacht's guest list with the exception of Harding, the Wards, and Kimber.

Willis, Ross, and Monty had discussed Harding as a suspect and had pretty much eliminated him from the list. As it turned out, Ross had met up with Jenny and Harry late that morning. When asked by Willis about their meeting, Ross related the following:

"When you left for the funeral parlor, I thought it might be a good time to interview the Wards. I found them in the lounge playing Scrabble. It turns out that both of them enjoyed word games as do I, so we hit it off right away and actually had a good time chatting over a game. Eventually I asked them how they knew Harding, and they mentioned that Ron, who is a top surgeon at the Cleveland Clinic, had successfully operated on Harding. in the past Harding had donated to the clinic, but after the operation he made a very large gift to the clinic. I got the impression that Harland had the couple on the yacht with the idea of perhaps making an even more significant donation, and that Harding wanted to know more about Ron and his work before he moved forward with this idea."

"When I asked the Wards where they were between the time that the last guest left and Ali's body was discovered, it turned out that they had left the yacht with another couple. They said that it had been such a fun party that they hated for the evening to be over. They were invited onto the couple's yacht for a nightcap. It was kind of a way of extending the fun of the evening. And they didn't leave the other couple's yacht until after 4:00 am. Little did they realize what they would return to… how the evening would end up. Sad."

"The Wards shared the fact that Ali was not well liked, "Not our type at all," Jenny had said. They particularly disliked how Ali had bragged to everyone about how much money she had won in the casino. Apparently, she left the casino with 7,500 Euros in winnings and boasted about it, to everyone's annoyance."

Willis made a note to find out what happened to the money she had won, as it wasn't on her and certainly not in her cabin. He also felt that while the Wards didn't have an iron clad alibi, they had been together mostly with the other couple, and it seemed highly unlikely that they would have had time to kill Ali, either together or separately.

At this same time, Monty tracked down Kimber, who was in her cabin writing a letter to her friend Fleur. While her cabin door was open, Monty nevertheless knocked on the frame of the door and when she looked up, he said, "I hope I'm not interrupting but would it be possible to ask you a few questions?"

Kimber covered her annoyance over the interruption, smiled, and said, "*S'il vous plait,*" as she gestured towards an armchair next to her desk. "I'm just writing a letter to my good friend Fleur. Yes, I know, writing letters is considered old-fashioned but Fleur and I go way back and this is how we correspond. Old habits die hard, as you Americans say." Monty came in and sat down, but before he could ask her any questions, she asked, "Would you mind telling me which twin I'm talking to?"

Monty smiled and said, "No problem, we get that all the time. I'm Monty. We are almost identical, but you can tell Ross by looking at his hands. He has a small blue dot on one of his fingers. Odd, isn't it?"

Kimber nodded her agreement and asked, "Now, what can I do for you?"

Monty paused and then grinned, as he was having trouble keeping his mind on his mission. He was distracted by Kimber's rather sensational looks. Seeing her in her bedroom and appearing very relaxed made it difficult for Monty to concentrate. He was finally able to focus and come up with the questions: "How did you happen to be here on this yacht and where were you during the hours between when the last guest left and Ali's body was discovered, roughly between 2:00 am and 3:30?"

"Easy, I met Harding at a party given by my best friend Fleur." She gestured to the letter she had been writing. "This letter is to Fleur telling her what has transpired here on the yacht. I'm sure she'll be fascinated. As for your second question: after seeing Harding several times, I was invited to be a guest on his boat. Little did I know what I was getting into."

"From what I understand from Harding, you were the first guest on the yacht. True?"

"*Oui*, I arrived first, and the others came the next day. I can tell you, it was all so nice and calm before the others showed up and things sort of started to happen."

"Did you see anything odd, anything out of the ordinary happen with conjunction to or with Ali?"

"Offhand, I would say non but wait... One afternoon I

was at the helm station and Phillip was explaining to me how to sail this yacht. You know, simple things like how to make it go right, left, and go in reverse and so forth. As we were talking, we overheard Ali having a heated dispute with Suzanne I can't really tell you what the argument was about, but as you Americans would say, it was all very hush-hush. But they were certainly very angry with each other. *Trés étrange*, I thought."

"Anything else you can think of that might be out of the ordinary?" Monty asked.

"Hmmm, not anything that comes to mind but if I think of anything, I'll be sure to let you know." Monty thanked her and left her to finish her letter.

Chapter Seven
What the Crew Had to Say

Willis, Monty, and Ross now concentrated on interviewing the crew. Willis wrote up the interview assignments as follows:

Willis would talk to:

Philip Molina—Captain

Suzanne Seyrat—Steward

Monty would talk to:

Olivier Tari—First Mate

Tony Blom—Engineer

Ross would talk to:

> Claude Seyrat—Chef and Head Steward
>
> Mac Mc Kinley—Chauffeur—lives off boat
>
> Colette Napier—Party Planner—lives off boat

Since the yacht was not at sea, the various workers on board had schedules that were fairly flexible except for Claude and Suzanne, who had to deal with getting the meals out on schedule plus keep the yacht in top shape. Willis chose to talk to Philip who, as captain of the yacht, was the major controlling factor in setting the rhythm of "Deeper and Deeper."

In his mid 50's, Philip was a man of few words; generally he was on the quiet side, but when need be, he was a man of action. When Ali's body was discovered, it was Olivier who had called the police, had taken some photos of her body as it lay in its pool of blood, and kept everyone out of the laundry room. He would prove to be invaluable in Willis's investigation.

Willis met Philip in the office, and he noticed that Philip appeared nervous, which apparently was unusual for him. He kept chewing on his upper lip. When Willis asked Philip if anything was bothering him, Philip fidgeted a bit and finally blurted out that he felt guilty about the laundry room. He said, "I'm responsible for the overall maintenance of the yacht and the safety of its passengers. The fact that the laundry room had a slippery floor due to some soap that had been spilled on its floor is inexcusable. That and not having a lock on that room... Well, I'd been meaning to put a lock on the laundry room but somehow never got around to it."

"Why would you lock a laundry room?" Willis asked.

"I suppose because I'm a cautious man by nature. But clearly what I should have done, I didn't do and that can't be undone." He said sadly. "I'm sure it was just a terrible and unfortunate accident. I fully understand that Ali wasn't a very agreeable person, but to kill her... That just doesn't make sense."

Willis had to agree with the man, and yet... It still seemed very suspicious. With that in mind, Willis said, "Thanks for your time and input, Philip. If any more thoughts cross your mind, you know, any ideas that might shed some light on what's happened, I'd appreciate it if you would share them with me. "

With that Philip nodded, shook Willis's hand, and returned to work.

Around that time, Monty cornered Olivier Tari and asked if he could have a word with him. Olivier was a handsome man who Monty suspected was about in his mid to late 30's. Deeply tanned, he had the look of a movie star. One of those action hero types. As the first mate and engineer, he obviously had spent most of his adult life sailing. He was lean and muscular, but the most pronounced quality about the man was he exuded an air of great confidence. That, plus his dazzling smile, made one feel comfortable in his presence. Once you got to know him better, it was clear that he knew his work and took pride in it. When Monty sat down with Olivier, he asked, "What exactly is your title and what does your work consist of?

"I have the fancy title of First Mate, which doesn't say much, does it? You might well ask what does that entail? Well, mostly I provide support for our captain, Philip Molina. We basically run the ship, making sure it and everyone on board is safe. It's a complicated job with a yacht of this size, a challenging but a wonderful job. I've been at this game for a long time and it's my hope that I'll be able to land a job as captain on a similar vessel in the near future. In fact, I have a strong lead for such a job starting in two months' time. I'll miss 'Deeper and Deeper' but it's time for me to move on."

Monty liked this man, but found that he was solely focused on his work and on little else, and after talking to him further, he concluded that the man had little to offer in the way of helping to shed light on the mystery at hand.

Later, Olivier tracked down Monty and said, "I forgot. The other day, I saw Lew rummaging around the galley looking for something. When I asked him if I could help him, he got very flustered and mumbled something about looking for a book he'd misplaced. I doubt that he was telling the truth. In any case, he quickly left. I thought it all very strange."

Monty then thought to himself, *Hmmm. Maybe I should have pushed Lew more and not just have assumed what appeared to be his total story was just that.*

Ross, in turn, had some difficulty cornering Claude Seyrat. Not that the man meant to be elusive. The simple fact was that he just was extremely busy as the Chef and Head Steward of the yacht. Getting interesting and appetizing meals out for seven passengers plus the crew was a huge job, especially since he took great pride in his work. Between himself and Suzanne, his wife, they were responsible for the food and the overall appearance of the craft, and they both took their work very seriously. He appeared to be in his late 40's, maybe early 50's.

Ross found out that Claude had worked on large yachts most of his adult life after studying the art of French cuisine at one of France's finest culinary schools. He was an interesting man with a strong, elegant look, was greatly valued and took great pride in his work. Unfortunately, like Olivier, he was a bit myopic when it came to life on board the yacht and was neither interested nor observant in the other areas of life on the 'Deeper and Deeper'. Knowing this from previous conversations with the man, Ross pressured Claude to talk about his job in the hope that he might shed some light on what had transpired over the last few days.

Despite pushing him for any pertinent details, Claude was less than forthcoming. Ross came away from his meeting with Claude none the wiser.

Later that day, Willis was able to get Suzanne aside, no mean feat as she seemed inordinately occupied with her many responsibilities. Being a partner to Claude, she was his right hand and as the steward on the yacht, she had many jobs, which covered supporting Claude in the kitchen and keeping the yacht in the best possible shape. Keeping up with the laundry and making sure the yacht stayed super clean was a huge and ever-demanding job.

Consequently, Willis had difficulty getting the woman to address his many questions. She simply was preoccupied. He was not sure if this was due to her workload or a means of keeping her distance from Willis and avoiding answering any questions. He found her to be physically attractive with a well-toned body, alert and strikingly handsome face, probably in her late 30's. She came across as strong and forceful. Probably a wonderful associate and friend as long as you were on her side, but Willis was not on her side, and he had a real problem in getting her to open up.

Willis was used to asking questions that got people to talk, such as, "How did you get into this line of work?" but when asked this question, Suzanne dismissed the question with, "I'm married to Claude," and that was all. She was obviously smart, tough, and evasive even with regard to the title of "married," as it was known that she and Claude were not legally married but had more of a common-law arrangement that apparently had been ongoing for a dozen or more years. Consequently, Willis left with basically no new leads.

Around that time, Monty found Tommy cleaning part of the deck. Monty said, "I wonder if I could talk to you a bit… I have a few questions."

"Shoot," he replied.

"Sitting around and talking is better than the work at hand."

"That's for sure. What do you want to know?"

"Well, for starters, how long have you been working on this boat?"

"Oh, I don't know… maybe four or five years now. It's a great job, but I have to tell you the pay is really not great. I keep thinking I'll get promoted or be offered a better job on one of the other yachts, but so far nothing. Kinda frustrating." He gestured around him as he said, "I know, it looks all so glamorous and it is, but for the passengers, not the crew. I definitely need to figure out a way to get ahead."

"Any ideas what you'll end up doing? Monty asked quite innocently.

"Not a clue, but believe me, I'll find a way."

Monty then thanked him and let Tommy get back to work.

Next on Monty's list was Tony Blom, the ship's engineer. As was usually the case, Tony was found working in the engine room. With its all-white interior, the room seemed devoid of any personality. As the heart of the ship, it was pristine and scrupulously clean thanks to the devotion that Tony lavished on it. When Willis admired the remarkable condition of the room, Tony thanked him with a smile that bespoke that of the pride and care the man dedicated to the functioning of the yacht.

However, when Monty continued with his complements, Tony suddenly changed his demeanor. It became clear that the man felt that he was grossly underpaid for his efforts and was seriously thinking of quitting. This surprised Monty, as Harding was considered to be an overly generous man and Monty wondered if perhaps this was a realistic case of underpayment caused by a lack of understanding on Harding's part, or was Tony just not being honest about the situation? Monty wondered if there might possibly be a need on Tony's part that caused him to feel that he needed more money. *Perhaps he's into drugs,* thought Monty.

At this same time, Ross wandered off the boat and went up to Mac, who was busy polishing the Rolls. Like Tony, Mac's whole life seemed to consist of polishing, caring for the engine of "his baby"… that, plus running errands for the yacht's occupants. Mac might have been helpful to Willis and his team, but Mac was somewhat simple and not very observant. In short, he drove and cared for the car like a parent with a special child and that was about it. In truth, he really didn't have much of a personality. The only sign that he might relate to others and have a sense of humor was when he was talking about how silent Rolls-Royces were supposed to be. Mac said, "The manufacturer claimed that when riding in a Rolls, the only sound you'll hear is the car's clock ticking. The reason for that is the clock is so damned loud... you'd think the directional is on… all the time!"

Chuckling at the thought, Ross left and looked for Colette. She, on the other hand, was bright and observant, and while she was not an occupant on the yacht, she had been around for several days setting up the party as well as being at the party. Consequently, she had some insight into the occupants and was quite willing to share her thoughts. After being assured by Ross that her comments would be kept totally private and not shared with the other people on the boat, she ventured the following comments:

"Harding West is a nice enough man… a man who knows very little about yachts but seems to be learning day by day. I like him a lot as he's fair, smart and caring. A very nice man."

"Kimber Lepelletier is someone I totally admire. She is tremendously smart, chic, and I think good for Mr. West. I like them together. I hope that this time on the boat will result in their cementing their relationship, but of course, one never knows."

"Lew Adelman, hmmm… poor man. Without Mrs. Adelman, he seems totally lost. What a shame. I think his wife was the glue that held the partnership together. I'm not sure he will do well in his line of business without her. He's a bit of an odd duck, don't you think?"

"As for his wife Ali Adelman, I know one shouldn't speak ill of the dead, but I strongly disliked her as she was a predator. From the moment I met her, I didn't trust her. I've known women like her before and they are evil and dangerous. I'm not a hundred percent sure but from what I saw, she liked men AND women. As soon as I found this out, believe me, I avoided her. No way was I going to let her get close to me."

"When it comes to Natasha, I have to say it's been an honor just to have met her. She's an international star, someone I've always admired. Now that I've seen her in a less than formal atmosphere, I have to say I find her rather sweet and not one to manipulate a situation. She doesn't strike me as being involved outside of her circle of dance except, of course, with Frans."

"I've spent some time with Frans and I have to say, I was quite surprised. I had thought he was one of those typical groupie types who latches on to a celebrity to get whatever benefits he can get out of the connection, but I don't know.

The man seems to have more depth to him the more one gets to know him. He's interesting, but seems to be spread thin and not focused on any one thing."

"As for the Wards, they are I think a fine couple… nice, agreeable, and fun. I find Mr. Ward to be remarkably bright, but then I can say the same about his wife. No wonder they have been together so long and seem to be very supportive of one another."

"Now for the crew: Are you interested in them?" she asked Ross, and his answer was: "Certainly. We need all the insight we can get."

"Understood" she replied. "This Yacht had some interesting characters."

"Captain Molina is a fine man and an excellent captain. He, plus the rest of the crew worked for the previous owners and I can't say enough about him. He's wonderful at his job… a good and kind man."

"Olivier Tari, the first mate, is quite the ladies' man. As you can see, he's handsome, but he's also smart and will probably end up being the captain on a similar boat as this in the near future. He'll do a fine job if and when he gets the chance."

"Claude Seyrat, our chef and head steward, is excellent at his job. At times his ego gets a bit in the way but that's what happens when someone takes great pride in his or her work."

Suzanne Seyrat is a different story. While she is very

good at her job, she has a quality that I don't appreciate in other women. At times she tries to be shall I say a bit… too friendly. I'll leave it at that."

"Tommy Leith, on the other hand, is fun and very nice. He also can sometimes try to get too friendly but in his case, it's flattering and he's pretty harmless… I think... I hope."

"Tony Blom, the engineer of the yacht, is pretty much a loner. He knows boats and is all-consumed by his responsibility in caring for the 'Deeper and Deeper'. I do get the sense that he's a bit envious of the passengers and their obvious wealth. I think he has trouble keeping his head above water financially at times."

"Now Mac is totally harmless in that his one love is that car of his. I would hate to be the recipient of his wrath if he found that I had in any way compromised the working of his beloved Rolls!"

"So that's about my take on the folks on or about the yacht. I hope it helps."

Ross in return said, "Thanks, Colette. You have been most helpful." He nevertheless thought, *That's all interesting, but there's one thing she said which might prove to be extremely helpful. I'll have to think about it.*

Chapter Eight
Death is Sailing on this Yacht

That evening while Harding and Kimber were out for a walk, Kimber made a suggestion. "I'm not sure if the timing is right, but what would you think of the idea of taking the yacht out for a couple of days? It would give us all bit of a break and possibly give some perspective as to what's been happening."

Harding thought for a moment and said, "I think that's an excellent idea. I've been really stressed out."

The next morning, Harding got Willis, Monty, and Ross aside and bounced the idea off them. Willis thought for a moment, rubbed his chin while deep in thought, and finally said, "Who knows. It might be a good idea. It might give everyone some time to kind of put things in perspective." Ross and Monty then nodded in unison.

Claude announced that he had plenty of food onboard and Philip said that he had filled the tanks the previous week, so they would have sufficient fuel as long as they were not going on an extended trip.

When Harding informed the guests that they were going to take the yacht out for a few days as kind of a break, everyone seemed to welcome the idea. Harry wanted to know if there would be Internet service, as he had some business he needed to address and was told that it would not be a problem. Lew was assured that they would only be gone for three, maybe four days. This break seemed to be welcomed by him. He proceeded to call the funeral home and explain that he was still working on plans for Ali's funeral. He, in fact, hadn't a clue as to what to do about her remains and so this delay was ideal for him… a welcome break.

That afternoon, after everyone had made his or her plans, all was set and "Deeper and Deeper" left the Yacht Club and headed out to sea. Everyone seemed to be in a celebratory mood… a collective sigh of relief was felt by all. Philip directed the yacht out of the slip and into deep waters. His aim was to dock near a small, little-known island which he felt would give everyone some privacy. Maybe those crazy Americans would want to swim nude or, at the very least, topless. He privately hoped Natasha and Kimber would comply.

The next day they arrived at the island, set anchor and settled in for hopefully a nice break. During the day, several of the guests dove overboard and swam a bit. Philip kept an eye on the guests who chose to swim but, to his disappointment, all the ladies kept their tops on.

Around 5:00, Harding's voice was heard over the ship's speakers, announcing in a mock voice: "Attention all crew members, attention all crew members, instead of the mandatory lifeboat drill, there will be an assembly on the aft deck of all passengers and crew where life support libations and hors d'oeuvres will be distributed to all."

This announcement was greeted with considerable enthusiasm, even a few cheers, and Lew was even seen to have a small smile on his face. Clearly all were worn down by the tension on board and to have the vessel move away from the dock created a sense that their troubles might be left behind… if not realistically, at least symbolically.

As everyone gathered, there was a great deal of chatter and laughter. Someone from the crew put on some salsa music over the speakers, which immediately added to the overall feeling of change, of relief that everyone seemed to crave.

Someone at the bar asked if anyone had seen the ice pick

but the question was ignored and soon Olivier was regaling everyone with jokes about ships. One that he told was:

"A beautiful New York woman was so depressed that she decided to end her life by throwing herself into the ocean. But just before she could throw herself from the docks, a handsome young sailor stopped her. 'You have so much to live for. Look, I'm off to Europe tomorrow and I can stow you away on my ship. I'll take care of you, bring you food every day, and keep you happy.' With nothing to lose combined with the fact that she had always wanted to go to Europe, the woman accepted. That night the sailor brought her aboard and hid her in a lifeboat. From then on, every night he would bring her three sandwiches and make love to her until dawn."

"Three weeks later she was discovered by the captain during a routine inspection. 'What are you doing here?' asked the captain." 'I have an arrangement with one of the sailors,' she replied. 'He brings me food and I get a free trip to Europe, plus he's screwing me.'"

"'He certainly is,' replied the captain. 'This is the Staten Island Ferry.'"

Everyone howled at the joke as they continued to drink and relax. It was so good to get away and to feel that maybe Ali *had* just had a terrible accident. After a while, Claude asked if anyone had seen Suzanne as he needed her help with preparing dinner. The rule was that everyone typically had drinks at 7:00 and ate at 8:00. It was now just a bit after 5:00, and he wanted to prepare something extra special and he would need Suzanne's help. When no one seemed to have seen her, Olivier said he would help Claude search for her.

Olivier was heard to say, "After all, the yacht, while spacious, isn't all that big." Olivier and Claude soon started searching the yacht, but going from cabin to cabin turned up nothing. Nor were there any signs of her on the decks or in the lounges. Someone suggested that perhaps she had decided to swim to the shore and go for a walk, but Claude felt that was highly unlikely. While she was an excellent swimmer and a very independent woman, she also knew her job and was very responsible... It was all confusing and a bit disturbing.

And so, at 7:00, everyone enjoyed the cocktail hour and Claude put together a fine dinner without Suzanne's help, which was at the table a bit after 8:00. Unusual for Claude. It was becoming an increasing concern that Suzanne seemed to have disappeared, as it wasn't like her to leave without letting Claude know her plans.

After dinner, Monty suggested that it might be fun to go ashore while it was still light out. The idea was met with great enthusiasm. In reality, it was Monty's thought that maybe they might catch up with Suzanne He was concerned that she might have hurt herself and needed help. And so, Tommy got everyone into the tender which was tied up to the back of the yacht and, after everyone was loaded onto it, he transported them to the shore. That is, all except for Kimber and Willis, who had decided that they would prefer to stay onboard.

It was generally hoped by all that Suzanne would be found. Claude began to believe that she probably had dived off the boat, swum to the shore and maybe took a nap, or maybe hurt herself and couldn't make it back to the Yacht. He was deeply concerned if they would find her.

In any case, some of the folks had taken towels and wore bathing suits.

When Lew was asked if he was going to take a swim with the rest of the folks, he relied "Don't I wish... To be honest I never learned how to swim and besides," as he tapped his large girth, "You don't really want to see a whale floundering around in the water even if he's just wading." Everyone laughed.

Kimber, because she had some letters to write, and Willis because he felt a certain unease that bothered him, had remained on the yacht. Willis was a man of instinct, and his instinct told him that something was wrong. Soon Kimber proved how right he was.

Kimber had taken a break from her writing and had wandered towards the back of the yacht with a pair of binoculars to see if she could see what the others were up to. The yacht was only 200 feet away from the shore, so she decided to not bother using the binoculars. As she went to put them down on top of one of the two WaveRunners. she had trouble finding a flat surface to place the binoculars. Both WaveRunners had white canvas covers to shield them from the elements. Simple fitted covers. Suddenly Kimber let out an involuntary gasp.

Below the one WaveRunner's cover she saw part of a person's body… a hand! She quickly found Willis in the office and wordlessly motioned for him to follow her. She led him to the WaveRunner and pointed downward towards the exposed hand. Together the two of them pulled off the cover and there was Suzanne, laid out across the machine. Kimber gasped and Willis grabbed her as a means of helping her feel safe, as the sight was incredibly disturbing. Suzanne's eyes were wide open with a look of terror on them, but while it was clear that she was dead, there was no sign of the cause. The fact that her body had been hidden under the WaveRunner cover made it clear that she had been placed there by the person or persons who had killed her.

Willis gently led Kimber away and then quietly said, "I have to get to work before the others come back. Will you help me?"

Kimber, who seemed incapable of speaking, solemnly nodded in agreement and Willis started taking photos of the scene. He then got a tape measure from his cabin and, with Kimber's help, diagrammed the location of the WaveRunner. The two worked quietly and carefully until Willis had recorded all the information he needed. Willis noted that there was a small puncture hole in the underpart of Suzanne's chin and realized that this is how she had been killed.

He also explained to Kimber that "Once the ship has returned to the Yacht Club, the police will take over and the yacht will most certainly be impounded. It is highly possible that everyone living on the yacht will need to vacate the boat and live elsewhere while the police investigate this murder. Ross, Monty, and I will be prevented from continuing our investigation. A messy problem at best."

Kimber and Willis then covered up the WaveRunner with Suzanne still on top of it. This time Willis made sure that Suzanne's hand was carefully secured so that it would not fall down and into sight. When everyone returned to the "Deeper and Deeper," Willis asked them to gather in the office to wait while he took Claude to his crew cabin.

When he and Claude reached his cabin, Willis said, "Please, Claude, take a seat. I have some disturbing news to tell you. While you and the rest were off the boat, Kimber found your wife. I'm afraid I have to tell you... She's dead."

Claude immediately said in a hostile tone, "I don't' believe you."

"I'm sorry but it's true."

"But how? Did she have an accident and where is she? I want to see her." Willis sighed and then responded with a simple "Come" as he gestured for Claude to follow him. He led Claude to the back of the yacht and when they got to the WaveRunner, he gently pulled the cover back to reveal Suzanne's body. She appeared to have had a violent death.

Claude gasped and turned away, crying, "No... No... No! Why? What happened?" Clearly Claude could not comprehend what had transpired.

Willis gently replied, "I believe she was murdered. Someone killed her and hid her body here under the WaveRunner's cover. Clearly, Claude was staggered by what he had just seen. He kept asking "How?" "Why?" "I don't understand." "You have to find the person who is doing all this!"

Willis had no answers for the poor man, and ended up gently walking him back to his cabin where he left Claude in shock and quietly sobbing. He asked, "Is there anything I can do?" Which, of course, there was nothing possible Willis could do. As he was leaving the cabin he thought he heard Claude mutter, "I warned her that she'd get into trouble."

Willis proceeded to return to his office where everyone was gathered and spoke. "I have some very disturbing news. While you were gone, Kimber and I found Suzanne" With that, everyone started to ask questions. "Is she OK?" "Where was she all this time?" and so forth.

Willis held up his hands to suggest that everyone quiet down. "I'm sorry to inform you that Suzanne has been murdered." There were audible gasps. The news of the murder affected everyone in different ways. Most were stunned but some were out-and-out scared. Who would do such a thing and who might be murdered next?

Lew commented, "I thought Suzanne had killed Ali as at one point I saw the two of them fighting, but I guess this changes everything. What… what the hell is going on?"

This was met with silence.

"It's our intent to find the killer or killers before we get back to the Yacht Club," Willis said. "We'll need everyone's cooperation, so if you see anything suspicious or have any thoughts that might help us, please come forward. Believe me, no thought can be too wild or appear too unimportant. Is that understood?" There were a few nods but mostly his words were met with confused silence.

Harding, in particular, was concerned that Kimber might be the next victim and urged Willis to agree to take the boat back to the Yacht Club as fast as possible. Willis, not being one to give up, insisted that they take two days to try to solve the murder. After everyone left, he and Harding took some plastic that was in the engine room, wrapped Suzanne's body along with some ice in separate plastic bags and stored her body in the laundry room with the air conditioning turned way up in an effort to keep her body from deteriorating.

When Claude later heard of this, he cleared his throat and insisted that he be the one responsible for changing out the ice from time to time so that her body would be properly stored and not decompose until they returned to the shore. He was heard to mutter under his breath, "It's the least I can do considering... " And his voice trailed off, leaving Willis to try to imagine what Claude was thinking. Willis made a steeple of his fingers and thought, *Was this a gesture of love or was he feeling guilty and trying to in some small way make amends for what has happened or... A curious question.*

Harding later found Kimber in his cabin crying. She was clearly very upset. He took her in his arms and gently rocked her until she calmed down. Finally, she murmured, "Would it be ok if I stayed with you here in your stateroom?"

He replied, "Of course," and hugged her tighter until she calmed down a bit.

Eventually, she said, "Do you remember, commenting about the number of locks on the door of my Paris apartment? Well, there's a reason for them. About four years or so ago I had someone break into my apartment. Luckily, I was visiting my friend Fleur and while the burglar didn't get much, he robbed me of something I hold very dear."

Harding could barely hold his breath.

"The burglar went through all my intimate clothing and did… how shall I say this? He made a personal mess and soiled some of my undergarments. Thank God he was gone by the time I returned. I cannot begin to tell you how disturbing this was. He robbed me of my peace of mind. I didn't sleep well for a week. Finally, I had all those locks installed. Now I need to move in here so I can feel a bit safe."

He replied, "I was going to suggest just that." After a considerable pause, as it was obvious that Harding was deep in thought, he finally said, "That's it. I won't take the boat."

"What are you saying? Won't take the boat? What does that mean?"

"I've actually just leased the 'Deeper and Deeper' with a contract that I would either buy the boat within a certain period of time—I think it's now maybe in the next 29 days or so—or I will forfeit the deposit I put down which I must tell you is quite hefty. But who cares?"

"There are too many negatives connected to this boat for me to ever enjoy it again. True, it is very expensive to keep up but that's not a concern for me. What I worry about is the bad karma surrounding this ship and, more important, I had wanted to share 'Deeper and Deeper' with you." There was a long pause and he finally said, "Quite truthfully, I am VERY concerned that you might be the next victim." He took her shaking body back into his arms and gently rocked her back and forth as if he was comforting a frightened child. "I want to keep you safe."

Later he shared his concerns with Willis, Monty, and Ross. When he mentioned to them that he had in fact just leased the boat and that he had decided not to finalize the purchase of the yacht Monty asked, "How much does it cost to run this boat?"

"Let's see." Harding reached into a file cabinet and pulled out a sheet that roughly showed the cost for running "Deeper and Deeper" for one year. "Hmm , that's odd. My gun that was on the shelf there is gone. Have any of you gentlemen seen it?"

There was no affirmative response.

Harding shrugged his shoulders and said, "Oh, swell, another mystery. Well, it'll turn up. Let's get back to this here cost sheet." And he read out the following figures:

Captain	$70,000.00
Mate	$60,000.00
Head Steward	$55,000.00
Steward	$40,000.00
Engineer	$40,000.00
Deck hand	$35,000.00
Medical & taxes	$90,000.00
Maintenance	$300,000.00
Total	$690,000.00
Insurance	$60,000.00
Fuel	$120,000.00
Dockage	$200,000.00
Supplies.	$150,000.00

Total expenses for one year. $1,220,000.00

Willis let out a low whistle in response.

Harding said, "Of course I had planned to offset much of the cost by leasing out the yacht, but I have a greater concern at the moment: I have a gut feeling, Inspector, that whoever is killing people on this boat might just be planning to go after Kimber next, God knows why."

"Kimber and I have spent a great deal of quality time together and I have to tell you that my feelings for the lady are getting more intense by the day. I have a great track record when it comes to gut feelings. I will do anything to keep her safe. Now, what can we do to safeguard her and everyone else until we get back to the Yacht Club?"

Willis replied, "My advice is to try to caution everyone and urge them to be on the alert. You're right to be concerned. This is an incredibly serious situation. Death is sailing with this yacht."

Chapter Nine
What Happened?

That evening, Willis had everyone from the yacht gather in the salon. Included were Jenny and Ron, Natasha and Frans, Harding, Kimber, and Lew along with the crew: Philip. Olivier, Tommy, Tony, and Claude. Neither Mac nor Colette had been on board so they were eliminated as suspects. Meanwhile, Ross and Monty were not there as they were quietly checking the various cabins using the excuse that they were trying to find Kimber's necklace which was missing. As they were checking Harding's office, they made the discovery that Harding's gun and the box of bullets had disappeared. Certainly, a big concern and yet when Harding was later told of the missing items, he seemed strangely unconcerned.

Back at the meeting, Harding took the opportunity to say, "Obviously, this business of two people dying on the yacht has been terribly disturbing and is the major concern of Inspector Willis here along with Monty and Ross. But there is also the upsetting fact that the fantastic necklace that Kimber wore at the party has gone missing. It was left on her dressing table after the party. I would appreciate it if the person who took the necklace would return it. Just please leave it on my office desk. No questions asked." Everyone looked around the room at this news and started discussing it amongst each other, but no one volunteered to produce that piece of jewelry.

Willis then asked everyone to settle down and started to explain how the investigation into the deaths was progressing. He started off by saying, "As you all know there have been two unfortunate deaths here on the 'Deeper and Deeper.' First, Ali died. Initially we weren't sure if her death was the result of an unfortunate accident due to a slippery floor or if someone had deliberately killed her. Then there was the surprise of finding Suzanne dead. At first, we were confounded, as there didn't seem to be a reason for her to be dead, and yet her body had clearly been stashed away on one of the WaveRunners. Today we found out what caused her death." With lots of murmurs, everyone looked expectantly towards Willis.

"Okay, everyone settle down. As I said, at first, we didn't see any cause for Suzanne's death's but after I had a chance to carefully examine her body, I found a small puncture hole under her chin. It appears that someone must have sneaked up behind her back and stabbed her with a small rod of some sort. ... Very unusual."

"We now face a delicate problem: if we were to return to Monte Carlo now, the police will take over. No doubt the boat will be impounded, and everyone will be required to leave the boat. While Harding here has graciously volunteered to put everyone up at the *Hôtel de Paris*, I suspect the police will take their time and ultimately everyone will want to leave and get on with his or her life. In short, the killer or killers might not be caught. That's why it is imperative to find out who the killer is and to do it fast!"

Willis then planned to interview the guests and crew one by one. The first person Willis met with was Tommy. While in the process of talking to him in the crew's lounge, Tommy offered Willis a soda, which he readily accepted. When Tommy opened the refrigerator, Willis asked, "What's that sticking out of the open champagne bottle in there?"

Tommy replied, "My mum used to say that if you put a silver spoon into an open bottle of champagne, the bottle wouldn't lose its fizz. During the party someone handed me that bottle which was opened, but then never got around to offering it to others, so after the party, I put it in the fridge along with a silver spoon and I just forgot all about it." Willis then proceeded to ask Tommy where he had been during the party, and he replied, "I was behind the bar practically the whole time of the party, as everyone knows. It was a very active party and I can tell you, those folks can really drink! I don't know if it's typical or if it was a question of people being in disguise and thereby acting out their character or maybe they're just a crowd that's big on drinking."

Willis carefully looked over the bottle. He soon discovered several hairs on it. He then took the envelope with the sample hairs from Ali and put it, along with the bottle, carefully in a box and later requested that Harding lock it in the boat's safe until they could return to port to have it analyzed. Willis knew that it would normally take days or even months to have the bottle and hair samples analyzed in the United States. Who knew how long it would take in France or Monte Carlo?

At the conclusion of Willis's interview, he thanked Tommy, walked out onto the deck and heard an unusual sound that cut through the normal peaceful solitude of the little island and its surroundings. It was the buzz of a helicopter that began to circle the yacht overhead.

Very strange...

The rest of the day was spent on board with everyone being very low-key. There was no swimming or diving off the boat, just everyone being quiet and introspective… in his own personal shell.

Later that evening Harding received the following email:

To Mr. Harding West:

We wish to inform you that thanks to our helicopter crew, we just received some remarkable photos of your yacht and the many passengers who have been part of some murders that have occurred on your boat. It is our intent to sell these photos and the volatile story of the two murders. One wonders how this will sit with you and your guests, including:

Natalia Dinara, Ron Ward, Lew Adelman, and Kimber Lepelletier?

Of course, these photos are for sale and we strongly urge you to be the highest bidder. We have potential bids from "The Star", "The National Inquirer," Real Crime" and "Murder Mysteries" as well as the London publication of "Hello". We await your response.

Harding wasted no time in gathering Willis, Monty, Ross, and Kimber to discuss this new twist. After showing everyone the email, Willis looked at Kimber and then back to Harding with sort of a "What's she here for?" to which Harding said, "Kimber is very much a part of my life now and I want her input, so I ask that she be included in all discussions from now on. Is that clear?"

Willis and party nodded their understanding while Kimber looked at Harding with surprise and a new awareness. "Now," Harding said, "Clearly someone here on board not only knows about the murders but is willing to sell the story for a price."

"Regarding the helicopter incident, obviously we have several options," Willis said. "One, Harding, you can bid to buy the photos and try to squelch the story, but there is nothing stopping them from taking more photos and even making up a fallacious story or stories. Two, you can ignore this threat and wait to see what happens. Three, you can turn this over to the authorities but, truthfully, who would these 'authorities' be? You're in a foreign country and it's doubtful if they would be of any help or even be interested in getting involved. Do you want my suggestion?" Willis asked, looking at Harding and then, remembering his comment about Kimber, looked over to her.

Without waiting for Harding to respond, Kimber said, "Why don't we gather all the concerned parties and ask how they feel?"

"An excellent suggestion," said Harding, and it was agreed that there would be an announcement made to the passengers that there would be an important meeting on the aft deck in 15 minutes. There was a brief discussion as to including the crew. It was decided that they might have some significant input. Clearly someone on board had contacted the folks who were trying to blackmail Harding.

Fifteen minutes later, everyone except Jenny was there. After about five minutes, she came rushing into the room with a towel around her head, exclaiming, "So sorry I'm late, I was washing my hair and as you can see, it still isn't fully dry," as she removed the towel.

Ah, women, thought Willis. *Always something!*

"Just to bring you all up to date," Willis began, "You probably are all aware that earlier yesterday, there was a helicopter circling the yacht. It turns out they were taking photos of us and are now threatening to sell the photos and our story to a gossip magazine." Willis gestured towards his partners and Harding. "What we want to know is: would you be OK with this leak, for lack of a better word… that is, should we just let the story get out or should Harding here try to pay them to keep the story quiet? For the record, I intend to find out who contacted these people. Someone here on this ship is leaking the story about the killings. If anyone has any idea who this person is, please let me know."

There were murmurs all around with everyone looking to see if they could spot the culprit.

Willis went on to say, "My suggestion to Harding is to ignore this threat and just let the story play out. Does anyone have a problem with this?"

At first, no one seemed to object, but Natalie and Frans were whispering together. After a moment, Natalie said, "Our first instinct was to be concerned about my reputation and my being involved in a murder scene, but Frans reminded me of the old adage that 'There is no such thing as bad publicity.' In truth, having my name in the papers can only hopefully help to extend my career."

Frans nodded in agreement.

"Okay," said Harding. "It's settled. I won't try to squash the story and we'll see where all this goes. Just let me know if anyone has a clue as to who's leaking stories to the press about our situation here on the "Deeper and Deeper.""

Later that day, Willis went to his office and found a large brown envelope. Inside it, wrapped with tissue paper, was Kimber's necklace with an apology: just one word pieced together by letters obviously torn out of a newspaper or magazine that were taped onto a sheet of paper and that spelled out the word "S-O-R-R-Y". He went in search for Kimber and found her in her cabin writing in her diary. He quietly handed her the envelope and when she felt the heft to the package, she smiled and removed the necklace along with the note. She tilted her head slightly, thought for a moment and then said, "*Trés curieux.*"

Willis replied, "Exactly. A mystery of sorts somewhat resolved but curious nevertheless." Willis looked at her and with a quizzical look on his face said, "Interesting that you've taken this necklace business rather calmly. I know that the necklace is a fine replica of an expensive piece of jewelry, but tell me, have you ever had anything of great value stolen from you?"

Kimber replied "*Non*, but I'll tell you a kind of an amusing story. A few years ago, I decided that it was ridiculous keeping my jewels at a bank on the opposite side of Paris from where I live, so I decided to move them to a local bank for convenience's sake. Now in my youth… or maybe not so very long ago," she said with a grin, "I had a very close friend… my paramour, well, yes, my lover. He was somewhat older than me and unfortunately passed away some time ago. Anyway, he had been very generous and enjoyed giving me some very valuable jewels… maybe roughly 1,800,000 to 2,000,000 Euros in total. While I hardly ever wear them, as they're kind of too youthful for me these days, I keep them because I cherish the memories they invoke."

"When I mentioned to the bank that I planned to take them out of the safety deposit box and take them to my local bank, they said, '*Madame*, we will send an armed guard with you when you transport the jewels from our bank to your other one.' I replied, 'That will not be necessaire.' What I did was: I simply dressed way down in a pair of old jeans and a worn sweater, and when I got to the bank, I put the jewels in a plastic shopping bag, took the Metro back to my part of town and secured the jewels in my local bank… Voila, all done!'"

Willis looked at Kimber in a new way…. kind of a mixture of awe and respect and maybe a bit of awareness that she could be a bit off the wall; that is, unpredictable but in a good way.

Harding called a buddy named Mal who was connected with the gossip publishing business. He assured Harding that he'd find out who was trying to peddle the story of the two murders.

Willis suspected that the culprit might well be Fleur, Kimber's best friend, as it appeared that Kimber was keeping her up to date on all the goings on. However, three hours later, Mal called and in his typically cheery voice announced, "That person trying to sell the photos and story is a guy named Tony Blom. Ring a bell?"

"Yup, loud and clear. Thanks so much Mal. I owe ya one."

"Ha! Forget it. After all the things you've done for me, consider us even." And with that, the two men chuckled and they both signed off.

Now what do I do? thought Harding. *I could easily fire him but he'd be difficult to replace on short notice and I really should find out why a seemingly nice, honest guy would be involved in something like this.*

And so, Harding discussed the situation with Willis and collectively they called Tony into the office.

When Tony came into the cabin, he appeared extremely nervous. He had a twitch in his eye and kept putting his hands in and out of his pockets.

Willis said, "Do you know why we called you in here?"

Tony bit his lower lip and hesitantly said, "No," and waited for the boom to be lowered.

"In that case, let us tell you," Harding said. "The other day a helicopter flew over the yacht and circled us a number of times. Do you recall that?"

No response from Tony.

"Well, that helicopter was taking pictures of the yacht and whoever it could find onboard, and I bet you don't have a clue as to why they would do that," he said sarcastically.

Tony tried to appear ignorant, but he failed miserably. In fact, he looked totally undone.

Willis jumped in and said, "Let's cut to the chase. We know that the helicopter was gathering photos to go into one of the gossip magazines and we know who set it up and who was going to divulge stories about what has happened here on the yacht. And all of fingers are pointing to you. Period."

Tony fidgeted and looked like he was about to cry when he said, "No, you've got me all wrong. I'm sorry but... I've been desperate. I need money and I need it fast."

"Why would that be?" asked Harding.

After a long pause and several false starts at trying to

attempt to explain himself, Tony blurted out, "My mum is ill and needs a serious operation on her heart and there is no money at home to pay for it. I was desperate and figured the one way that I could make some money fast was to tell people what was happening here on the 'Deeper and Deeper'. I know it's a betrayal of your trust."

Having said that, he decided to go for broke and blurted out, "And just so that you know, the amount that you pay me is pretty damn small. It works fine for someone who takes a job like mine on a lark and is trouble-free, but really, the pay is pathetic, especially if one runs into trouble like my mum needing an operation and needing it fast."

"Really" said Harding guardedly, with a glance toward Willis. "I actually don't know how much you get paid."

"Well…" Tony thought for a while and then got up the courage. "Let me tell you. As your engineer I get paid $40,000 a year. That's a measly amount, sir. And yes, I know that there are all sorts of fringe benefits such as free housing and meals and such, but in the long run if one has an emergency, one is without resources. That said, I was desperate, and it seemed like an easy way for me to get some money fast."

Willis, who had a paternal but a gruff side as well, said, "So tell me, Tony, if you were willing to sell us out to the gossip magazines, what else are you capable of doing? Murder perhaps?"

Harding added, "And I don't suppose you know what

happened to my gun and the box of bullets that was on that shelf behind you?"

With that, Tony started shaking his head "No... no!" and the shaking quickly moved to the rest of his body as he was clearly VERY upset.

This young man was either the greatest actor ever born or was in fact very upset about his situation. Harding thought for a while, and after whispering into Willis's ear and getting a nod from Willis, he said to Tony, "How much will your mother's operation cost?"

Tony replied in a hopeless voice, "The equivalent of a year's salary for me."

Harding walked over to his desk, took out a checkbook, made out a check and handed it to Tony. "Now, call your gossip contacts and tell them that you were mistaken and there is no story here. We'll talk later about your salary. I just want you to realize that if I were to raise your pay, in fairness to the others, I would have to raise everyone's pay, which might not be possible. Let me see what I can do. No promises. Meanwhile this business of my paying for your mother's operation is between you and me. Understood?"

Tony was clearly staggered by what had just transpired and looking at the check, kept shaking his head in wonder. He finally stammered "I understand. Thank you... thank you very much, sir." and left the cabin.

Willis said to Harding, "Are you sure about this? That's

incredibly generous of you… if the story about his mother is indeed true."

Harding replied, "I'm 75 percent sure Tony has told us the truth, but I'll have his story checked out. If the reality is that Tony killed those two ladies, then the check will put him off guard and that will have been a reasonable amount to pay for getting to the truth."

Interesting approach, thought Willis. *Not my way of operating, but interesting.*

Willis then asked, "Tell me, Harding, are you always that generous?"

"Well, I try to be caring and considerate of my fellow man. How about you?"

Willis was a bit taken aback by the question, but gestured for Harding to sit down and, after scratching his chin for a moment, proceeded to say, "There is no way that you'd know this, 'cause I never talked about it, but back in high school, my mother died when I was only fifteen years old, and my father was pretty much a failure as a parent. He was judgmental and less than supportive to me as I was growing up. As you may or may not know, I'm divorced and have no kids. Maybe that was meant to be and possibly a good thing. I don't know. I'm getting on and I can honestly say after my divorce I've been pretty soured on the marriage bit. No kids… no attachments. However, through some rather extraordinary events, I met Ross and Monty, and they have in a way become my surrogate family… my kids. They're smart, interesting, and wonderfully supportive and I love 'em."

Harding looked at Willis in a new light. They both shared this one thing in common. They both were divorced and were trying, each in his own way, to create a family. Willis with his boys and Harding with Kimber. Both men nodded to each other, and a new bond was established.

"I have to say, Harding, that I don't think it was a good idea to leave that gun of yours on that shelf in plain sight. Has it somehow disappeared? I'd hate to see someone hurt."

"Oh, I wouldn't worry too much about that."

This did not sit well with Willis, but he decided that the man must know what he was doing... He certainly hoped so.

Chapter Ten
A Revelation…The Results

The next day Willis gathered the ship's guests and crew together at the helm of the yacht and announced "We're getting very close to the Yacht Club and also to solving the question of who murdered the two ladies. Interestingly enough, I believe that there were actually two killers." With this everyone looked first at Natasha and Frans and then also at Harry and Jenny.

Willis now had everyone's attention. "As you're all aware, when we reach the Monte Carlo Yacht Club, the boat will be surely impounded unless we, of course, have solved these murders before we land. I have been in contact with some forensic folks, and they have come up with some very interesting information."

Ross looked at Monty. They both looked puzzled, since Willis had said nothing to them about a forensic lab. They both turned and looked at Harding, who shrugged at them, as if to say, "I know nothing about it."

Willis continued, "First, I had a champagne bottle tested. It was my theory that the bottle had been used to hit Ali on her head, causing her to bleed to death. The bottle was definitely the murder weapon, as it had a few hairs on it that matched Ali's, plus some blood which we are still checking… but without a doubt, is certainly hers. Two people and just two people had handled that bottle. The first set of handprints showed that Tommy had held the bottle in a normal manner." With that everyone looked at Tommy with a new sense of curiosity.

Willis went on to say, "The other set of prints showed that a person other than Tommy had held the bottle in a manner in which it would have been used as a weapon to swing downward and hit Ali on her head. That person is Suzanne Seyrat." Everyone now looked at Claude who looked stunned and upset.

Willis said, "It is my conclusion that Suzanne killed Ali by hitting her over the head with the champagne bottle in a downward motion, hitting her on the top of her head and then leaving her to bleed to death on the laundry room floor." As he said this, he took a bottle which he had previously taken from the from the bar and demonstrated how one would swing the bottle downward. It was a rather violent gesture and it made Willis's point dramatically.

"Our suspicion is that Ali and Suzanne had a sexual liaison that had gone bad. So the next question is: who killed Suzanne? At first Ross, Monty, and I thought it must have been Claude when he realized his wife had been involved sexually with Ali." With this, Claude looked incredibly upset. Willis continued. "But some new evidence came up that showed that he's innocent. After studying the evidence, everything points to Lew as the culprit."

Lew looked at Willis askance as though Willis was out of his mind. Willis ignored this and went on to say, "Suzanne was killed by having a sharp rod jammed up the underside of her jaw. This is consistent with the type of killing that is taught in the branch of service that Lew here was trained in. He was taught to take out an enemy by sneaking up behind that person and jamming a sharp rod up under the victim's chin so it would enter the skull at the jawline. Some of you reportedly saw Lew using an ice pick with a vengeance on the ice bucket the other day. It is my bet that he jammed that up into Suzanne's skull, killing her, and then stashed her body on top of the WaveRunner after throwing the ice pick overboard. Isn't that so, Lew?"

A smile crept over Lew's face as he said to Willis, "Well now, aren't you the clever one!" He pulled out Harding's handgun and said to Harding, "That was awfully careless of you to leave your gun in your office in full view and even with a supply of bullets. Really stupid and careless of you."

With that, he aimed the gun at the whole group and said, "I think it's time that you all join Suzanne." There was a terrifying moment as some of the group interpreted Lew's remark as everyone was going to die like Suzanne.

"No, I'm not going to kill everyone. You're all going to be locked up down below until I make my escape. That is, everyone except Harding and Kimber here, who I have other plans for."

Gesturing toward Philip, he said, "Philip, leave the boat running and aimed toward the Yacht Club." He then marched everyone at gunpoint down into the laundry room and said, "Before you go in there, drop your cell phones on the floor outside the door over there." He said gesturing with the gun. "Now everyone, except Harding and Kimber, get inside there and don't try anything smart or you'll soon find out that the army trained me to be a crack shot and you'll regret it."

When everyone was inside the laundry room except Kimber and Harding, Lew said, "Now lock the door, pick up those phones, and get up those steps." When they reached the top deck, Lew demanded, "Now, throw those cell phones overboard."

As they did this, Kimber looked at Harding frantically and Harding said under his breath, "Stay calm, don't worry." Kimber looked at Harding as though he was certifiably insane. Lew proceeded to march Harding and Kimber at gunpoint to the rear deck. Chuckling to himself, he said sarcastically to Harding "OK, Mr. Money Bags, we're approaching the Yacht Club. We all know that docking this yacht will be a huge challenge for you in that you'll surely fail, as clearly you are not much of a sailor. It will be great fun to watch you smash this boat into the dock, but I assure you, you will land this boat any way you can so that I can then get off after I take care of the two of you! I have disliked the two of you immensely. You especially, Harding, what with all your grand exhibition of passing out money at the Casino, having that ostentatious party, showing off how filthy rich you are… not to mention your oh-so-cozy relationship both on and below the deck with Kimber here."

"This is a wonderful chance for me to teach you a lesson, to get even. I assure you that it didn't take long for me to figure out that Suzanne had begun a volatile relationship with Ali, and that when things quickly soured with their sick relationship, Suzanne took things into her own hands and decided to get even with Ali. God knows why. I've never understood women, and dykes in particular, but clearly Suzanne decided to get Ali and get her good. I hated

Suzanne for killing Ali as Ali was my whole life. The two of us were fantastically successful partners. In essence when Suzanne killed Ali, she killed my career, and so I took great pleasure in eliminating Suzanne in turn."

"I had been incredibly upset ever since we went to the funeral home to see Ali's body. So now it's 'get even time'. Harding, I want the pleasure of seeing you witness your beloved Kimber die in front of your eyes."

Staring at Harding with diabolical hatred, he said to the two of them "Now get over there," as he gestured with the gun for them to move further to the back of the boat. Kimber was so terrified she could hardly move, while Harding was his usual cool self. When they finally got to the stern, Lew continued.

"It was delicious how Suzanne struggled as I pushed that ice pick up under her throat and into her brain... just like the good old days when I was in the special armed forces." As he patted his breast pocket, he said, "Oh, and by the way, thanks to you, Harding, I have the 7,500 Euros in my pocket that Ali won at the Casino which will come in handy when I make my escape."

He then looked at Kimber who was cowering behind Harding and said to her, "Step aside Harding... are you ready to die, Kimber?"

Kimber tightly shut her eyes and cried out, "Harding, help me!"

Lew, with a maniacal grin on his face, said, "Here we go, Kimber: one, two, three!" and he pulled the trigger. There was a loud sound as the gun fired, but Kimber wasn't hit. Lew said, "What the fuck?" and pulled the trigger again and again only to hear more shots but with no results! At the same time, Harding lunged at Lew and pushed him off the back of the yacht. Kimber, seeing that the boat was about to crash into the pier, raced toward the helm station, and remembering what Philip had told her about the basics of operating the "Deeper and Deeper", grabbed the controls, but it was too late. There was a horrific crash and splintering of wood. Kimber threw the engines in reverse and the boat backed off the pier and over Lew, killing him instantly. The water turned red with his blood as the 7,500 Euros in various bills floated up to the top of the water.

Kimber, who was still breathing heavily and shaking violently, said to Harding, "I don't understand why... why wasn't I shot?"

Harding smiled with that mischievous grin of his and said, "Remember how you were after me to get rid of that gun as you hate guns so much? Well, instead of getting rid of it, I simply put it out of your sight in my office where you never were inclined to go, along with a box of blank cartridges which I ordered online. I thought that whoever was the killer might steal the gun along with what he thought were real bullets. That way no one could get hurt. Didn't keep Lew safe now, did it?"

He then said, "Please, go down and get the others out while I try to keep the yacht from doing any more damage to the dock." But it was too late. The yacht, having crashed into the pier, caused a considerable amount of damage to both the dock and the boat. Within moments, a shaken but smiling group came up on board, including Philip, who immediately tried to secure the boat. Soon after, the police showed up and Willis and Harding filled them in on what had happened while some other policemen worked at fishing Lew's body out of the water.

As predicted, the boat was impounded and Harding, at considerable expense, canceled the contract on the yacht and left it to the lawyers and the insurance company to work out the costs of the damages to the boat and dock.

Epilogue

Everyone was held for a few days before the investigation was concluded.

Harding put everyone up at the *Hôtel de Paris* and eventually they were released by the police. Philip and Tommy consequently had paid vacations. Olivier, who had a strong lead for obtaining a position as captain of another yacht, was facing a bit of a wait, so Harding paid for his hotel as well.

Claude moved on to another job that did not include sailing, as he had his fill of yachts. Tony went home to care for his mother and Mac was quickly snapped up by the owners of an even larger yacht than the "Deeper and Deeper".

Before everyone split up, Harding arranged for a farewell party in a private room at the *Hôtel de Paris*. Harding had gathered Harry, Jenny, Frans, and Natasha, the crew, including Mac, and also Colette, and especially Willis, Ross and Monty, who Harding referred to as "the guests of honor." He had asked everyone to dress up, specifying that the crew should wear their best uniforms. In short, he had indicated that the party would be a very dressy affair.

And so, everyone gathered in a room on the second floor of the hotel. Once everyone had assembled, one of the hotel employees circulated with a tray of champagne. Ross mentioned that Kimber was not present, but Harding sort of just brushed the thought aside with, "You know women, never on time. I bet she has a great excuse this time!" After a short period, Harding announced, "Will you all please put down your drinks and join me through that door over there?"

He went over to the door and opened it to reveal a large, elegant room that had white Chiavari chairs set up in several rows. At the end was a huge arrangement of hundreds of white roses and assorted white orchids that covered the entire far wall. The site was stunning. Off to the side was a woman elegantly dressed who was playing a harp. Harding went down to the center of the wall of flowers. When he reached it and he was joined by Philip. When everyone was seated, a door in the back of the room opened to reveal a beautiful woman who carried a bouquet of lavender orchids that matched her dress, as the harpist began to play "Here comes the bride."

As the lady was halfway down the aisle, Kimber stepped into view dressed in a breathtaking white gown and a smile to match. There were many murmurs and smiles as it became clear they were about to see Harding and Kimber get married. Harding had earlier checked out Philip, to make 100 percent sure that he, as a captain, was legally able to marry the couple, as not every captain is legitimately allowed to do so. After it was confirmed that he could lawfully perform a marriage, he proceeded to do just that as everyone beamed, especially Willis, who—along with a few others—had a tear or two in his eyes.

After the wedding was over, Harding, who was all smiles, directed everyone towards a side door which led into a sizeable room filled with a large oval table covered with a white crisp tablecloth and sprays of white orchids. There were place cards for everyone, with Harding sitting at the head of the table and Kimber seated to his right, and the lady in lavender—who turned out to be Kimber's best friend Fleur—to his other side. Ross and Monty were seated next to Kimber, and Willis was seated to Fleur's right. Willis was immediately engrossed in a somewhat intimate conversation while Ross and Monty looked on with amused smiles on their faces. After an elaborate supper, the meal was topped with a beautiful multi-tiered wedding cake.

As everyone was finishing their cake, Harding tapped his glass of champagne, and when he had everyone's attention, said, "I have a toast of sorts. Before everyone goes his or her own separate ways, I want to thank my wonderful friend Inspector Willis, and his terrific partners Monty and Ross, for their incredible contribution in helping us safely get through an impossibly difficult situation on the 'Deeper and Deeper'. Without them, who knows what would have happened?"

He then he looked at Kimber and said, "Well, in a way I guess this is more of a statement than a toast. What I've learned during our time together is an important lesson which I hope will bring Kimber and myself even closer, if that's possible. You all know the old adage that the best two days in a boat owner's life are the day he buys his boat and the day he sells it. Well, this is a new version: the best day is the day that one learns that boating is not meant for certain folks, including yours truly. It is safe to say that none of you, including Kimber and myself, will ever set sail on the 'Deeper and Deeper' again. No loss there. To all I say, 'Good safe travels wherever you go and God bless!' I trust Kimber and I will have many years together free of boats and the problems that come with them."

Raising his glass of champagne, he smiled and said, "Here's to my extraordinary wife who, without question with each passing day I will love deeper and deeper."

To come:

Duplicity, Care to Die?
An Inspector Willis murder mystery

About the Author

Ray Klausen has had a wide and varied background ranging from being a top television and theater set designer for over 400 productions, including nine Broadway shows and 10 Academy Award productions, resulting in his winning three Emmy Awards. He has worked with such celebrities as: Michael Jackson, Prince, Cher, Bea Arthur, Barbara Streisand, Madonna, and Elvis, to name a few.

His previous book, *Behind the Scenes: From Hollywood to Broadway,* is a remarkable history of the television theater world from the late 1970s to the early 21st Century. Previous novels include: *Duplicity* and *Duplicity in 3 Acts.* Both are "An Inspector Willis Murder Mystery".

Also by Ray Klausen
Published by Amarna Books and Media

www.ingramcontent.com/pod-product-compliance
Lightning Source LLC
Chambersburg PA
CBHW060450310726
48977CB00001B/381